"All right. W... married:

"I'm pushing forty. My mother would love me to get married. I expect I will buckle under social demands and get married sooner or later, so why not now? The usual mid-life crisis, really."

"You expect me to believe that?"

He sighed. What would it take to satisfy her? The truth? He doubted it. But what would she do if he told her that he hadn't slept one solid night since he'd laid eyes on her? That he hadn't known such violent sexual attraction was possible, that it made him wonder if it was a symptom of a breakdown of some sort? That all he could think of when he had a moment to himself was how it would feel to have his body buried in hers, his senses full of her taste and his head full of her cries of pleasure?

She'd probably run screaming.

Dear Reader

For me, writing has always been a delight that nothing else surpasses, an escape into a world where anything can and does happen. A world that I create and control. How magnificent and satisfying is that? My characters are real people to me, people I laugh and cry with, live and love with. I also love pitting them against impossible odds, both in the world around them and inside their hearts and souls. They really have to earn those happily-ever-afters I end up giving them.

As well as writing, I love singing, painting, reading in every genre, and keeping fit. And besides sharing my life with my characters I'm blessed to share it with my wonderful, supportive family and friends.

There is nothing better.

Olivia Gates

Recent titles by the same author:

DOCTORS ON THE FRONTLINE

EMERGENCY MARRIAGE

BY
OLIVIA GATES

MILLS & BOON®

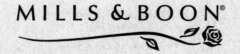

This one is for you, Mom.
For believing in me, for being there for me,
and for everything that you are.

First published in Great Britain 2004
Harlequin Mills & Boon Limited,
Eton House, 18-24 Paradise Road, Richmond, Surrey TW9 1SR

© Olivia Gates 2004

ISBN 0 263 83923 0

Set in Times Roman 10 on 11¼ pt.
03-0904-55401

Printed and bound in Spain
by Litografía Rosés, S.A., Barcelona

CHAPTER ONE

"LAURA—you fool!"

Laura Burnside almost dropped the arms of the woman she was dragging along the ground.

Freezing, eyes darting around the chaos, heart shaking her apart, she sought the source of the furious shout.

Someone's shoulder slammed into hers, jolting her back.

Concentrate, Burnside, all her senses screamed. *It doesn't matter who's calling you or calling you what. It can't be* him *anyway. Get out of here. Drag that woman away…*

Another outburst of shots. Another man fell a few feet away from her. No way to help him, not now. One victim at a time. Bending again, tightening her grip on the woman's wrists, she dug her heels in and pulled. Much heavier than her, getting heavier with every inch. Pain stabbed her side again.

Fool. That was what the voice had called her. *His* voice. It couldn't be him, of course. What would he be doing here, in Buenos Aires, hundreds of miles away from his home and work? His rage must be reaching out to her all the way from Santa Fe. No one disobeyed Armando Salazar.

It could also be her mind calling her a fool, using his voice. And it would be right. She'd gotten herself into this, thought she could do it. It was amazing what looked plausible—not to mention how a mind could stray—in a desperate situation…

Violent purple with sickening yellow blotches exploded behind her eyes. Someone's forehead had rammed her left cheekbone. She staggered, letting go of the woman's wrists, colors fading to gray. She held herself still as her consciousness wavered, drained, willing light and colors to come back. If she succumbed, let herself be KO'd, it'd be over for that woman. For her.

Another body, then another collided into her, fists and feet plowing into her gut and shins. She was the only one going against the tide, and they were sweeping her backwards with them in their blind escape path.

In the uproar, her own angry shouts reached her ears as if from a distance. The woman. She had to get back to her. She didn't know how, but she made it.

Just as she bent to her again, a thundering *"Laura!"* drowned even the cacophony of human shrieks and gunfire.

It *was* him.

Her head swung instinctively, violently, looking for him in the stampede. The next second a missile whizzed by her head. A fist-sized rock thrown with all the strength and fury of someone deranged by oppression and desperation. If not for his shout, it would have smashed her skull.

Then he was there, materializing above her, face grim, wings spread, filling her vision.

This is how Dracula—no, Batman—must look. A little voice inside her made the ridiculous, untimely observation. *Swooping down on his quarry, staggering, scary even to those he saved.*

In the next heartbeat he snatched her up and under the protection of his massive body. It was almost a surprise to realize his spread wings were not a cape but a jacket, held up to block rocks that were falling short of their targets, pelting them instead.

"Don't— *No…*" She resisted him, desperate to return to her casualty. He only swept her higher. Her feet kicked air.

Her fingers dug into his arm, his chest, anywhere, trying to gain his attention, to regain her freedom. "Put me down, Salazar! That woman—she'd been trodden on—and those two men…"

She was talking to his jaw as he plastered her to his side, running with her to… *Where* was he going?

The idiot man had taken them right into the thick of the riot!

Her breathing stopped as the masses battered them. She'd rushed to the woman when they'd started receding, forced back by the police forces, when she'd thought she'd had a chance of pulling her away. It had been scary enough, dangerous enough then. She had the bruises to prove it. But now—being right in the middle of it all...

Dread smeared her vision gray and red. Huge and strong though he was, no way was he a match for this mindless crowd. He was starting to stumble, her weight no doubt hampering him, compromising his balance.

"Put me down, Salazar!" This was no longer indignation. This was survival. If he didn't, he'd soon be brought to his knees. Then they'd both be trampled to death.

"Shut up, Laura!" He swung her around to face him, forcing her thighs around his waist, one large hand clutching her buttocks, the other a steel harness behind her back, carrying her like she'd once carried her baby brother and sister. "Hold on—tight!"

She did, clamping her legs around him, clinging for dear life. Not that she needed to. He crushed her if he were trying to hide her inside him. Her flesh felt battered into his, her breath took in his heat and sweat and anger.

Her senses sharpened, receded. Fear and anger and awareness dragged her under. She made herself surface, frantic to see what was happening around her, where he was taking her. One eye's field of vision was all she managed to free. The hundred and four jarring steps she'd counted had delivered them from danger and to one of La Clínica's beat-up ambulance vans.

One violent yank brought one of its double doors crashing back on its hinges. Expecting to be thrown inside with the same vehemence, she braced herself. The next second she couldn't hold back her surprise at his extreme gentleness as he deposited her on the paramedic bench. Her eyes darted to his face. Nothing could have been harsher.

So what else was new? Ignore him.

Impossible to do that, as usual. Especially now, with his bulk blocking her view. Then he moved, followed her inside, and she could finally see the woman they'd left behind. She and the other victims were still motionless in the middle of the street. The mob had veered into a side street, some persistent elements still going back to pelt the police forces, provoking more warning shots.

She'd made a lousy call before, going out there before the riot had receded enough. Now there were only the police in the background. If they made a run back for the victims, shouted that they were doctors, they could reach them, carry them back. She measured the distance, gulped down a steadying breath then moved. Armando moved first, shoving her down again. No gentleness this time.

"*Por Dios*, get down and *stay* down! I didn't risk getting my head smashed in to get you off the street just so you'd dash out again and succeed in getting yourself killed."

She would have ignored him now if she wasn't losing the wrestling match with him. Better luck wrestling with steel handcuffs! Impotence and fury crackled on her lips. "What kind of doctor are you to just leave victims behind, Salazar?"

"*I'm* not leaving anyone behind, but *you're* staying put!" He hauled a hard collar and a rebreather mask with an oxygen reservoir from the shelves lining the ambulance walls, sprang from the van, slammed the door behind him and locked it with the remote control.

For a few moments rage threatened to burst her skull. How *dared* he? What made it OK for him to run back out there and not her? And he couldn't possibly carry them all! What was he trying to prove? That he really *was* a superhero? What was his special power, Latin chauvinism? Just because he'd managed to swindle her out of her position as aid operation leader…

Blasts erupted again amidst a new uproar, startling her out of her fury. This time nature joined in, then drowned the human frenzy as a sudden, violent downpour started pounding the van. From the rear window she saw another horde, this time bigger, tens of thousands turning the corner of the main street and heading for the police forces. And in between there was Armando, carrying the woman and leaning over one victim, then the other.

Seconds stood between him and being squashed in the middle of the mob. And he was wasting them!

Buy him time. The thought screamed in her mind.

She flopped back on the stretcher, prayed that he'd armed the van's alarm system by locking it and rammed both feet into the rear window.

She didn't even hear her own shouted '*Yes*'.

The siren blared, jarring enough to cause the antagonistic sides' momentary hesitation. A hesitation Armando used to rouse one of the fallen men by pressure on his forehead, to shove him out of harm's way and, with the woman held high in his arms, to squeeze between the two waves of hostility before they collided.

Laura returned her attention to the door. How the hell did that doorhandle work? She'd definitely unlocked it but the handle just wouldn't budge. Frustration roared in her ears, seethed from her lips. "Dammit—damn *you*, Salazar!"

She had to get out, meet him halfway, help him. *Yes*—the oxygen tank!

The window withstood the first swing, fragmenting but holding up. A cry of rage and a second swing made a big enough hole for her arm. In a second she'd worked the handle from outside, got out and was already running to him—only to watch him lurch over the woman in his arms.

His name was torn from her. *"Armando!"*

He'd been shot. He'd die.

God, please, no, not again*!*

Her feet pounded the hot, wet tarmac, every step shattering a pool of rain and transmitting a bolt of agony to her right side, a reminder of how close she'd come to dying herself. She didn't care. She had to reach him, save him…

He fell to his knees, chest heaving, still clutching the woman. Laura's heart stuttered and stopped for the moments it took him to struggle back to his feet, hauling the woman in a more secure grip, staggering onwards. Her heart was hammering again, almost bursting with a brutal mix of confusion, dread and hope. There was no blood on him—but if he'd been shot in the back, she wouldn't see it. Were they shooting real bullets now?

Had he or hadn't he been shot?

A hundred feet away, his hoarse warning hit her, explaining everything. "Tear gas…" Then he succumbed to a fit of uncontrollable coughing.

So that was it. In his exertion he must have gulped deep of the irritant chemical. Like breathing in fire…

The next second, her instincts kicked in. She couldn't risk exposure too. She ran back to the van, as far away as possible from the incapacitating fumes that she could now see rising, even among the sheets of rain pounding down on the combatants. But in their desperation to escape, the mob was getting even more dangerous, spreading towards Armando in nightmarish tentacles.

But he was ahead, fast and strong and heading to…

Oh, God, where *was* he going?

He was no longer heading in her direction. He'd end up in the middle of the riot again, the way he was blindly… But of course! He was blind. His eyes must be burning, profusely tearing, lids squeezed shut with blepharospasm—beyond his ability to open them again.

Her mind raced. Rushing out to lead him back was out of the question. One way, then—she had to be his eyes. If he could hear her frantic shouts over this nightmare…

"Armando—turn right! *Right!*" He stopped. He'd heard her, thank God. "Make a ninety-degree turn. A bit more. Yes, *yes*—that's it. Keep going in a straight line now. Faster. There's a sidewalk in about twenty paces. I'll shout to you to stop before you reach it." She had to stop then, to catch her breath, grind her teeth. Every shouted word was lancing a hot arrow into her chest and abdomen.

"Stop!" He did, still heaving with racking coughs. She forced more directions out. "Just one more step and you'll hit the edge of the sidewalk—yes, you're there. It's high, more than a foot. Yes, yes—now four of your paces and you'll come off it. No—watch it!" He stumbled off the sidewalk and fright forced the air out of her. He straightened, his body language hesitant and anxious as she gasped for oxygen, fighting against the mounting pain. She failed in both but still shouted, "It's all clear to where I'm standing. Just follow my voice."

In twenty seconds he'd stumbled to her and she took some of the woman's weight off him, directing him until they had her on the stretcher. She harnessed her in, then turned to him.

His face was drenched in tears, his nostrils flaring convulsively, his eyes spasmed shut as tears gushed down his cheeks and off his hard jaw. Every inhalation shrieked in, and came out in frightening barks of abrasive coughing. She pushed him through the doorway leading to the driver's compartment and shoved him down in the passenger seat.

Rushing back to the patient compartment, she snatched a look at the mayhem outside. The man Armando had roused had stumbled out of danger. The other casualty, whom he'd managed to drag aside, hadn't. She had to rush to him.

She kneeled by their casualty, prying off the rebreather mask Armando had placed on her face. It would protect her against the tear gas.

Armando's labored words carried to her, and a jolt of horror paralyzed her in mid-motion. "He's...dead. Rubber bullet...through the...eye."

She knew so-called 'safe' rubber bullets could cause considerable damage, according to the distance they were fired from and the area of the body they hit. She hadn't known they could kill.

Now she knew.

Urgency bubbled over inside her. *Help those you can.*

She reached for Armando, shook him. "Keys, Salazar."

He only pointed to his right back pocket, almost coughing his lungs out again. Moving his convulsing, massive body was almost impossible. She was pummeling him in frustration by the time she had him supine over both driver and passenger seats. Now to fish the keys out. Her fingers felt like wet spaghetti and his jeans—were they painted on or what?

Get those keys. No time to think where you're shoving your hands.

At last she succeeded. Too late. The mob's sentinels had reached them. One pulled the driver's door open, jumped in, shouting in Spanish at her. A blind need to protect surged inside her, blanking out the pain. She leapt over Armando, rammed the man back, snatched the door from him, slammed it shut and central-locked the van.

Time slowed. Her mind raced. Everything was suddenly in pinpoint focus, one thing filling her awareness.

Get Armando and the woman out of here.

In a vacuum of calm, she shoved Armando back in his seat, jumped into the driver's seat, fired the engine and put the van in motion, showing the mob who were now battering it with their fists and ramming it with their bodies that she wasn't about to let them stop her or enter it, yet still managing to give them enough time to move out of her way.

It was street after street of that. Suspended in reaction, she drove on and on until her path cleared. Then she floored the pedal. Armando's choking curses rose as his unrestrained body bounced off hers then slammed against the door with every violent pitch. Strange—her mind didn't register that she was driving roughly. Then his harsh wheeze filtered to her above the screaming engine noise. "*Stop.* Far enough…"

How he knew that with his eyes closed, she didn't know. She had no idea where they were. All around were the rolling plains of the magnificent pampas, only a few cars on the horizon of the near-deserted road.

She slowed down, pulled up off the road, eyes flying to the clock.

Unbelievable.

Only thirty-five minutes. From the moment her cab had refused to go any further when the riot alert had broken out, leaving her to reach her destination on foot, and she had gotten mixed up in all that.

She turned to Armando. His coughing was abating, but his lips were blue with oxygen deprivation and his eyes were still spasmed, tears still pouring.

"Water…in…the back…"

She understood. To counteract the effects of tear-gas after removal from exposure, eyes, nose and mouth had to be copiously irrigated with water or saline. In seconds she returned with four bottles. He made an urgent gesture demanding she hand them over.

"Shouldn't you be breathing easier by now? Maybe a bronchodilator…"

He twisted a bottle open, choked, "See to…our casualty…"

He was right. Simple triage made their casualty the priority. She left him rinsing his eyes and went to the unconscious woman.

Laura snatched a look at the woman as she turned on the suction/aspiration and wall-mounted oxygen outlets, snapped on gloves and chanted under her breath, "A, B, C, D, E."

As a surgeon, she usually didn't get to handle the ABCDs of emergency resuscitation, but they'd been so deeply ingrained in her during her early training, they were second nature. Mentally ticking off the procedures, she simultaneously and seamlessly implemented them.

Thrust jaw above hard collar to overcome upper airway obstruction. Suction excess secretions in trachea. Gather equipment for intubation. Ventilate with one hundred per cent oxygen. Assemble laryngoscope, lubricate cuffed endotracheal tube, cut tape, ready clamp, syringe, flexible introducer and forceps. No need for induction anesthesia since the patient was already unconscious. No gag reflex. No need for local either.

In seconds she had the woman intubated, the tube connected to the bag-valve combination and was ventilating with oxygen. She looked at the chest. No improvement in air entry. She reassessed her measures, made sure the ET tube was in place in the trachea. It was. Airway secure but breathing not any better; shallow, strident 55 prm.

Exposing her patient's chest, she saw the tell-tale paradoxical movement of her ribs, a segment moving in while the rest moved out with breathing. Flail chest—ribs broken in a row and moving independently of the rest of the chest wall.

Stethoscope already drawn, she gave the chest a listen. Normal breath sounds on the right side, none on the left. On percussion, stony dullness at the base of the lung. Hemothorax. But the trachea was deviated. Probably hemopneumothorax—both blood and air gathering around the left lung, collapsing it and interfering with the right lung and heart function. Fatal if the building air and blood weren't evacuated—fast.

She picked an angiocath to perform a needle thoracostomy, slipping it between the ribs and into the pleural space. She heard the distinctive rush of air in relief, then placed a one-way valve on the end of the angiocath to prevent air re-entry. Immediately, there was an improvement in air entry, if not in breath rate.

Check circulation. Pulse 180—ectopics all over the place. Blood pressure 80 over 50—hemothorax must be massive. *Going into shock.*

She exposed the woman's arms, snapped tourniquets on both and inserted two wide-bore 14-gauge IV cannulae. The woman moaned in protest around her tube.

''Sorry I had to prick both arms!'' She released the tourniquets, hung two Ringer lactate solution bags from the IV holder, connected their tubing to the lines in the arms, set the drip to maximum, then swooped for tube thoracostomy instruments to drain off the blood. First, local anesthesia.

"This sting you'll thank me for," she said soothingly as she injected the local anesthetic and disinfected the area until it took effect.

"I doubt she…understands a word of English—if she can hear you at all…"

Laura started. Armando—she'd forgotten he was here.

"She'll understand my tone, that I'm taking care of her!" She snapped her eyes back to the instrument compartment and extracted a 38-French large-bore chest tube, explaining why she needed it. She looked him over as he came to crouch beside her. "So you're better now?"

"Better than you. Move—I'm doing this."

She protested but he'd already snapped on gloves and was taking the scalpel and tube out of her hands. He wasn't breathing much easier, but *she* was sweating. Not the stuffy sweat expected with the heatwave that was ending March, Argentina's last summer month, but the cold, sick sweat of depletion. Bright pain had settled in her right side. Gray mist had crept up over the rest of her a couple of times back there. He was probably in better condition than her. She made way for him.

Flopping into the attendant's seat, she watched him recline the cot so that their restrained patient lay in a 50-degree reverse Trendlenburg position with her legs down. Both that and the incision between the ribs in the mid-axillary sixth intercostal space made for best drainage of blood. In deft, sure moves, he punctured the intercostal muscles and pleura with a curved hemostat clamp, advanced and secured the track with his finger and inserted the tube into the pleural cavity. Blood gushed out, just as she'd predicted. He secured the tube with a suture and tape and connected it to an underwater-seal bottle, attaching it to the suctioning device.

She busied herself with a secondary assessment of the woman's vital signs. Breathing down to 24 and blood pressure up to 110 over 70. Measures working. She told him. He nodded. "Let's look her over," he said.

Apart from a multitude of bruises, a quick exam for dysfunction and a full exposure didn't reveal further significant injuries. Eyeing the bottle for the collected blood, Armando frowned. It was over 900 ccs.

"A lot," she said.

He gave a slight shrug. "But it has almost stopped coming. She'll be OK. Load me 10 mg diazepam while I decompress her stomach."

"But her GCS is 5—6 at best!" Centrally depressant drugs were contra-indicated when consciousness was compromised and scoring on the Glasgow coma scale measuring responsiveness and alertness was below 8. "How can you consider sedating her?"

"I believe she lost consciousness with respiratory distress and shock, not from a head injury. If you hadn't noticed, she's lightened up."

"What if she has? Why not just let her wake up, extubate her and put her on positive pressure ventilation with a face mask?"

"She's a cervical spine injury suspect. If we need to operate further, and it turns out she does have a cervical injury, this ET is our one safe chance of having one in. I want it left in."

Laura mulled this over, watching his every move as he slipped in the nasogastric tube and emptied the woman's stomach. Incisive, ultra-efficient.

And right.

Damn him.

In seconds, she'd slipped the diazepam into the woman's drip, hooked her to the cardiac monitor and raised her head. She found him watching her in turn, something like surprise in his bloodshot eyes.

He shook his head, made a strange, wheezy sound—an incredulous laugh? "Good work!"

He *was* surprised, double damn him! How dared he be surprised?

But really, why should *she* be surprised? She should be used to his opinion of her medical competence, of her worth in general, by now.

Still biting her tongue, she watched as he checked their patient one last time, then rummaged for a syringe, loaded it with an ampule diluted with saline and injected himself subcutaneously.

"Ventolin," he rasped, then muttered something else under his strident breath.

So he did need a bronchodilator and… What had he said? It sounded too much like Laura *Loca* to her. Crazy Laura.

"*What* did you say?"

"So you heard me, huh?" His shrug was careless as he crossed to the driver's compartment, throwing a calm "Good" over his shoulder.

In seconds he was revving the engine loudly and putting the van in gear, forcing her to scramble to the passenger seat.

"*I'm* crazy? I'm not the one driving a car fifteen minutes after being zapped with tear gas."

"One of us has to and apart from my eyes stinging like hell and my skin and lungs feeling about to combust, I'm in a far better condition than you—Laura *Loca*!"

"You're saying it again!"

"Don't mention it. What the hell do you expect? What did you think you were doing, running out like that? Was reporting me such a desperate priority that you didn't mind risking your life to do it?"

"Reporting…? Listen here, Salazar—"

"No, *you* listen here, Laura *Loca*. You didn't have to sneak behind my back. You wanted a report delivered to GAO's central liaison office, I would have delivered it for you myself, even if you'd painted me black in it, even if you'd lost me GAO's backing. And no matter what else you think of me, I'm your surgeon and I, and only I, say when you can leave your hospital bed. When I do, it won't be so you can go on another death-defying escapade. This one almost got me killed. Your last one *did* manage to kill Diego!"

CHAPTER TWO

"NOBODY asked you to come after me!"

And nobody had asked Diego either. She'd told him she'd had nothing more to say to him. But he'd intercepted her. Just giving her a lift, he'd insisted. He'd tricked her, again, had been so confident he'd talk her out of leaving, seduce her into forgetting what she'd come to realize. He'd been incensed when he'd failed. Then he'd crashed the car.

"And *my* death-defying escapades?" She hissed her outrage at the blatant lie. "*Diego* was driving, if you remember! Without a seat belt. And he almost killed me, too."

"My point exactly. Yet you walked out today as if all you'd suffered a week ago was a sprained ankle, and not a lacerated liver and abdominal aorta with a hemothorax and intraperitoneal hemorrhage to make our patient's here look like a minor leak. I won't even mention your facial wounds, or the ten units of blood we pumped into you, or the six-hour operation to gain hemorrhage control—"

"It was only a limited laparotomy."

"Only? Oh, yes, you were damned lucky. But don't be so smug. That I didn't have to open you up from your neck down was a piece of luck that, along with surviving today, used up all your luck—for this lifetime at least. You walked out of hospital today against every rule in the book."

"You removed my drains three days ago. It was perfectly all right for me—"

He interrupted her again. "Every moment you're on your feet you're compromising your healing, inviting complications."

"Early ambulation is good for healing," she objected.

18

"Ambulation as in getting out of bed, walking around the room then getting back into bed."

"I'm a surgeon myself, no matter how you might like to forget that, and if I feel anything alarming—"

"If you don't listen to reason, you might still *die*! You do know how many complications can set in, don't you?"

This morning, she'd been confident she'd been well enough to discharge herself, against his orders. But that had been then. She hadn't expected to be sucked into a nightmare. The sting of every ram and blow she'd suffered was a grim reminder of yet another catastrophic miscalculation. Complications were now a definite possibility. She'd concede that. Just not to him.

When she kept her face averted, he grated on, "How about another slow leak of blood into your pleural cavity, turning into a clot this time? Or a bath of pus that only a thoracotomy will empty? Do you want your chest opened from side to side? Your sternum sawed open? You want to have a scarred lung or a chronic, debilitating respiratory infection? I won't even mention the complications from renewed abdominal bleeding... *Por Dios!* I can't believe we're having this conversation! You did go to medical school before you became a 'surgeon', didn't you?"

He growled under his breath and pressed harder on the gas pedal. "Quit playing the heroine, Laura. No one's snapping photos now. Or will there be another press release soon?"

"A press...!" That was it! The antagonism she'd felt towards him ever since she'd laid eyes on him erupted. "You may have gotten used to doing and saying anything you please, to flaying and bossing people around—certainly Diego, and me too when you wormed your way into GAO's good favor—but now I'm—"

"Now *I'm* up to here with daredevils, Laura!" His usually dismissive, cool black eyes flashed something unknown, harsh and hot. Their inflammation added a sinister effect as his bronzed, powerful fingers chopped a sharp movement. His daunting body and singular looks created an impression that was overwhelming. With his wet, tousled hair and livid darkness, he was downright intimidating. Not that intimidation featured in the chaotic feelings he provoked in her. "And if I'd had that kind of power over Diego, he'd probably be alive today," he continued.

"Oh, so it wasn't me who got him killed, then? Or do you only mean you'd have banned him from knowing me, the reason for his death?"

Something flitted in his eyes. Her eyes narrowed, trying to catch and nail down the elusive expression. He snatched it out of her reach with an exhalation and a turn of his head. "That was out of line."

What? The infallible Armando Salazar admitting to a transgression? And to her? That had to be another first. Adding to every other world-shattering first she'd had in Argentina. Her first lover. Her first command. Her first break-up. Her first car crash, emergency operation and riot. And now the first thing that sounded like an apology from the man who'd been the common factor in it all.

"I was—still am—furious with you, but that's no excuse. It *was* an accident, and no matter where your relationship was at the time—which is no business of mine…" He stopped, tossed her a turbulent look. "*Infierno*, Laura. You're not dragging me into a pointless dissection of the past. You're going back to La Clínica and this time you're not walking out before you're fully healed, even if I have to chain you to your bed."

Anger spiked. "Well, let me tell you something, you—"

"I lost Diego, Laura." His forceful baritone was so unexpectedly, so unbearably soft, it had her retaliation sticking in her throat. "He slipped through my fingers and I couldn't save him. But I saved you, and I'm damned if I'll lose you now!"

Something hard tumbled in her chest. What was that in his steel eyes? Pain? The juggernaut who played as hard and fast as he worked, who swept everyone and everything aside and did as he pleased, actually had…feelings?

For the three months she'd been in Argentina she'd been

busy avoiding him, then resenting him. In the past few days, she'd been battling death then emotional turmoil, desperately seeking closure. It never occurred to her to look through his eyes, feel his turmoil. Diego had been his cousin, more of a younger brother. And he'd died in his hands.

And he *had* saved her. Not that she couldn't undo all his efforts. The pain in her side was sobering—frightening even. It was pointless, childish, arguing with him when he was right. And he did make her feel childish, stupid.

The need to defend herself to him rose again, and this time it wouldn't be denied. "I never intended jeopardizing myself, but I couldn't ignore the victims."

His laugh was furious. "That's probably the one thing I'm not angry with you about. It was stupid, unbelievably so—but it was very brave. I didn't know you had it in you."

Don't rise to that. He expects it.

What the hell. She'd satisfy him, the callous creep. "Oh? You mean I wasn't after another photo and headline?" He grimaced, shrugging away his earlier maligning words. "What the hell do you know what I have or don't have in me? What gives you the right to pass judgement on people—just who do you think you are?"

"I'm your surgeon, that's all I am right now. And I may not know you, but can you deny you've had way too many photos in magazines and newspapers since you arrived?"

"It wasn't me as *me* all over those pages. It was me as so-called head of Global Aid Organization's Argentina Project. And it wasn't even a GAO initiative. It was your local newspapers that developed that unhealthy interest in me and my team, and I'm damned if I know why!"

Armando knew why all right. Couldn't believe she didn't. She was too tempting to the paparazzi. The dazzling American surgeon, turning her back on her family's riches, throwing away a lucrative private practice in the US to come to Argentina, devoting herself to humanitarian work. Add that to the trendy hook of her online romance with Diego and the stunning sight they'd made together…

He hadn't had the stamina to look at newspapers lately. He would bet, with the accident and Diego's death, interest in her must have spiked to fever pitch. And if they found out she'd risked her life to save riot victims…

"And I wasn't in Buenos Aires to report you."

Her forceful statement jerked his attention back to her. His gaze slid off the road and over her. Took her all in. Glossy, rain-straight hair, the perplexing blend of black, blue and indigo, pulled into that down-to-her-waist, unflattering braid. The unique bone structure and drained tan of a face that spoke of her brush with death. Bluish-yellow bruises, spreading like leaking ink stains from beneath her dressings. Lips, usually dimpled, flushed bows, now a taut, colorless line. And eyes. Those eyes! Sooty-lashed chameleon emeralds, now murky jades set in fragile purple. A body that had gone from luscious to almost skinny.

And she still sent his hormones raging.

He swore.

"Boy, I knew you were…many things. I'm adding plain crude to my list!"

"Your Spanish is taking off if you understood that."

"Swear words are a must-know-first in any foreign language. A universal defense against locals who enjoy insulting you to your face, counting on your ignorance!"

"That was a strictly inner debate, not intended for your ears. Sorry I blurted it out loud."

Her eyes lightened, becoming emerald again with suspicion. "It's too late to pretend, Salazar!"

"I agree. It *is* too late. You've called me Armando at last, so you can't go back to calling me Salazar."

"I used to call you *Dr.* Salazar, and I called you Armando…" She stopped, shook her head, looked away.

"Only because you thought I'd been shot," he completed for her. "I always did wonder at your insistence on calling me Doctor, even when we were meeting socially, daily, when I'm on a first-name basis with everyone. You are, too. Why do you find it so hard to say my name?''

Was the man for real? He didn't realize she'd rather not call him anything, not be near him at all? That he made her feel defensive, vulnerable, useless?

That first time Diego had dragged her to Armando's house, to show her off to ''the Salazar patriarch'', Armando had taken one look at her, one hard, drawn-out, enervating look, then, thankfully, had dismissed her. He'd looked at Diego as if he'd lost his mind, getting mixed up with her. He hadn't said anything, though. A month later, he'd made it equally clear he thought GAO crazy to give her the aid operation reins. This time he'd done something about it.

One day she'd been head of GAO's mission in Argentina, the next, for all intents and purposes, his subordinate. He'd swooped in and snatched it from beneath her feet, then shoved her out of the picture.

He wasn't only local and a medical jack of all trades, a surgeon/emergency doctor/search-and-rescue operative all rolled into one; he was also director of La Clínica— Argentina's most revolutionary medical facility. He'd established it after Argentina's financial collapse had torn apart all systems, the medical system being the paradigm of disintegration.

She'd met Diego when he'd been in the US recruiting medical personnel for his cousin's project. And before she'd met him, she'd thought it the most exciting, enterprising medical endeavor ever. If it hadn't been for her previous commitment to GAO, she would have loved to have joined herself.

But then she *had* met him.

It had all gone nightmarishly wrong. Coming to Argentina was supposed to have been the start of her new life—the love she'd never had, the work she'd always dreamed of and people who really needed her. So many expectations, so much advance work and plans.

But no amount of logistics or fantasies could have prepared her. Not for the reality of the situation at ground zero, or for the meteoric deterioration of her relationship with Diego. She'd needed time. To sort out her mess with Diego. To start becoming effective in her job.

But Armando had denied her that time. He'd talked GAO's administrative body into making La Clínica GAO's base of operations in Argentina. And in La Clínica he made his own rules and dispensed them with an iron hand.

He stopped at nothing to achieve his goals. Distorting truths, manipulation, outright lying. He hadn't needed her team's expertise as he'd said, he'd only needed GAO's resources. In the month they'd been in La Clínica, he'd totally excluded them and was dispensing GAO's resources whichever way he pleased, throwing its agendas and protocols out the window. No wonder he felt he deserved to be reported.

What infuriated her more was her own reaction. She'd taken his abuse lying down. It didn't make her feel any better, wailing that her personal mess had drained most of her stamina. An excuse worse than the offense. Weak, foolish, stupid!

But it was over now. Diego was dead, and her love for him long before that, and she wasn't needed in any other way here.

Time to put her expertise in cutting her losses to use.

"Well?"

So he was still waiting for an answer! "I'll call you whatever I like, not what you like." Her words were cool, tight. "And I will continue to recuperate. Just not at La Clínica."

"Oh, no?" He slowed down and shoved his face closer to hers. Space shrank and air disappeared. "Where else will you have your operating surgeon, the only one really qualified to follow you up? To handle any complications that may yet develop? To remove the stitches all over your face? Or do you intend to do it yourself back in your villa before your posh welcome-home party?"

An involuntary hand went to her facial dressings. "I can remove my own stitches."

"Even the ones you can't see without the help of a mirror?"

His persistence finally wore her nerves down. "Don't you understand? I don't want to dwell on my injuries, on the accident, on…on… I want—I *need* closure."

"Who doesn't? But you think you'll ever have it if you have scars to remind you every time you look in the mirror? Maybe every time you take a breath?"

"I'm sure you did a great job putting me back together, that there'll be no complications…"

"Is that your informed medical opinion, *Dr.* Burnside?" His generously shaped lips twisted, and suddenly she felt something new towards him. The need to physically strike out at him. To wipe off that abrasive superiority written all over him.

Stupid urge. You can't afford more of those. Just shut him up.

She breathed in. "Listen, if anything happens, I'll seek immediate help. But right now I'm not going to La Clínica. Not as a patient. Haven't you demoted me enough already? I'll just get on with my life. I don't need your permission to do that."

His fleeting, severe look hit home. Then he spoke the three words, slow and distinct, "Yes, you do!" A few strands of his hair caught the sun that had bleached them copper as he took a turn into a road she recognized, the road leading to Santa Fe and La Clínica. "Going back for your full post-operative period is non-negotiable, Laura."

"I—"

"Drop it."

Staring ahead at the boundless horizon she was still unused to, she fell silent, stymied.

Armando heard her frustration loud and clear. He kept his still-scalding eyes on the demanding road, slowed down some more. She'd been battered too much already.

"So how bad am I beneath these dressings?"

Her subdued question surprised him into biting off, "Bad enough!"

He caught a more-than-crude expletive back at the last moment.

Why had he said that?

Oh, what the…? It was just as well. She had to face the reality of her injuries, didn't she? And anyway, at the moment her injuries *did* look bad. And they could remain so if she compromised her recuperation. Laura *Loca* Burnside, philanthropist extraordinaire, glittering, brilliant society darling, who had no idea just how dangerous and desperate it really was here.

The moment he'd learned she'd left, he'd predicted she'd head for GAO's headquarters, smack dab in the middle of the city center the riots were ravaging. He'd never driven so recklessly. All the way, Diego's accident, his death, haunted him, taunted him. He could have ended up the same today, chasing after her.

But in either case, she *hadn't* asked either of them to…

"Anything more specific to add to that delightful and sensitive report of my impending metamorphosis into a monster?"

His attention snapped back to her. Was that sarcasm? She had a sense of humor? He'd thought she took herself too seriously. She'd never cracked a smile, not in his presence. And he'd been present almost all the time she'd been in Argentina. Her glares were something, though. It was almost a surprise he hadn't turned to stone. Parts of him had…

He was really losing it! If her resentment affected him this way, he didn't want to know what a smile, a touch would do…

Stop it, moron!

He inhaled. "You'll see for yourself when I remove your stitches."

"I must be really mangled if you elected to do a primary

repair of my facial wounds during a life-saving operation, risking extending the already dangerously long anesthesia time.''

He had been aware of that danger. But he'd weighed everything—her condition while on the table against the risk of the wounds healing by secondary intention, raising the probability of scarring. He'd felt it safe to go ahead.

So why was the unfamiliar urge to justify his decisions to another, to her, riding him—again? Her eyes on him had always made him feel this way. Ever since he'd laid eyes on her—the last thing he'd expected Diego's new woman or GAO's mission head to be.

He tried to stifle the urge as usual. He failed this time. ''For best esthetic results, you know it's optimum to close wounds within eight hours of injury.'' Wasn't it enough to feel defensive? Did he have to sound it, too?

She tilted her head, her braid sliding with an audible thud to her right shoulder. He tightened, ached. He'd never had it this bad. Then she gave him a strange look—a skeptical one?—and his heart, his hands, itched.

''If the patient isn't stable enough, if it's in any way risky, primary repair could be delayed by as much as seventy-two hours without significant change in esthetic outcome.''

''*Significant* being the operative word here. Scars might seem *in*significant to you now, but later they will be. Trust me.''

''I trust my clinical experience. I used *significant* as a figure of speech. In my experience, delayed repair—with proper wound occlusive care—yields the same esthetic result.''

''You mean I should've waited until you revived from anesthesia, then put you under again while you were recovering from major trauma surgery and even more vulnerable? Not to mention that I couldn't predict how your post-operative period would go. What if you'd deteriorated? For long enough to lose the golden time window for primary repair?''

''You know you could have done it under local.''

"I'm sure you would have appreciated the extra joy of local anesthetic jabs in your condition!"

"I wouldn't have minded a few nerve blocks, and I *would* have preferred to be awake while you worked on my face."

"Why? Did you want to hold my hand through it?"

"And why not? Maxillofacial surgery was part of my *six-year* surgical residency. I might have given you a few tips on how to handle facial soft tissue injuries."

His foot eased off the gas pedal and the car almost slowed to a standstill.

He'd suspected there was more to her than the sullen, haughty façade she projected. So was this at last the real her? All that fire and diamond-sharp toughness?

Whatever confrontations she'd tried to kick up with him before, she'd done so in arctic reserve and infuriating polite-ness. It had all been about who was supposed to be in charge. There'd never been implied criticism of his professional or surgical prowess before. Implied? Hell, there was no impli-cation involved now. She was *telling* him he'd made a lousy call, combining her procedures, that his surgical judgement stank.

But was she lashing out at him for thwarting her plans, for dragging her back? Or was it the stress of trauma? Or had her orders and his connection to Diego kept her from expressing her opinions, opinions she now felt free to voice?

All of the above, most probably. Not that he cared what she said to him or thought of him. She was letting go of the tight reins of social propriety and professional diplomacy and let-ting the real her shine through.

And it delighted him.

Delighted him? *Now?* The tear gas must have left him more oxygen-deprived than he'd realized!

"Why did you stop bickering with me?" One sable eye-brow disappeared in mockery beneath her bandages. "Sty-mied?"

"I don't 'bicker'. And I didn't know there was a contest going on."

"No? Then why do I have the distinct feeling that you've won again?"

"*Por Dios!* Won what? What is there to win?"

"The last word, as usual. You're a control freak, aren't you, Salazar?"

He closed his eyes, begging for control. This couldn't be happening to him. Every time she called him Salazar in those cool, low velvet tones, lust kicked hard in his loins. Just the memory of her crying out his name when she'd thought him injured—the fantasy of her crying it out, again and again, in another form of desperation...

Cool it, Salazar. No time to discover you're having an early mid-life crisis rolled in with a second adolescence. This is probably the one woman on earth who should be off limits.

He ventured a look at her. Her uncanny eyes were gleaming their challenge. He groaned. "I guess right now, if I say it's for your own good, you'd send my head rolling."

"Don't tempt me. I don't have enough energy to knock your head off."

"You're angry with me."

"Go to the head of the class."

"Well, if you want to bawl me out, you'll have to stand in line."

That stopped her, deflating her unnatural animation. She slumped down in her seat and averted her face.

"See what I mean? The last word. You just have to have it. I didn't think you'd stoop to spouting nonsense to score it, though."

"It's not nonsense. You can't even begin to understand how angry I am at myself. I failed Diego and he died. La Clínica is still lacking in critical care, and it's my responsibility. It's also my responsibility you walked out today. I just see that beating myself up over mistakes and oversights is futile and counter-productive at this point. I'll just have to live with it. At least I'm alive—and strong and healthy as an ox.''

"Don't! Patronize me, ignore me, or even overrule me like you've been doing so far. But don't—don't you just sit there and tell me you're feeling guilty. I don't want to hear about it.''

So she was feeling guilty, too! But was it just a natural reaction to surviving an accident that had killed another, or was there more to it? Had she played a more active role in that accident, as he'd accused her? Shouldn't she be feeling more than guilt, with her lover dead? Though Diego had said he'd broken up with her before the accident. Was that why she wasn't grieving for him?

So many questions, all answers less than pretty. Not that he cared. He just wanted to slam on the brakes and haul her into his arms, comfort her.

Yeah, sure. Her only comfort right now would probably come from giving him a black eye!

He wrestled the urge down, adding it under an airtight lid to every other wild desire she provoked in him. "Try to sleep, Laura. There's still a long way ahead.''

He watched her eyes dull with resignation, watched her turn her head on the headrest and fall silent.

He'd said there was a long way ahead.

Did she know how long yet?

Laura jerked awake to a jarring lurch. Aggravation rose inside her. Just as she'd managed to doze off, too, with the jostling motion of the van and Armando's nerve-racking presence beside her!

But he was no longer beside her. He was beneath her. At least his lap was, his hot, hard thighs cushioning her head and shoulders, her upper torso hanging in the air in the space between their seats. Her lips and nose were buried in his abdomen's steel-ridged muscles, in his virile-scented, *naked* flesh.

Breath congealed in her throat, the urge to jackknife up and away from the heart-stopping contact overwhelming. She twitched and the powerful hand securing her in place tightened around her buttock. A whimper escaped her swollen lips.

He shifted to accommodate her more and her right breast molded against his splayed thigh. As for where the back of her head was pressing…

She pushed at him and he immediately removed his arm.

"You're awake."

"How perceptive." She forced herself to sit up in a natural, unhurried movement. "And you're naked!"

"I'm not."

Oh, no? Then she must have developed X-ray vision, if she could see the daunting expanse and definition of his exposed chest and abdomen. She'd known he was first and foremost a thoroughly physical being, tough, vigorous, carnal. Those were the first things anyone noticed about Armando Salazar. She hadn't needed to see him naked to figure that out. But now he was…

"I'm half-naked," he concluded lightly.

And I'm half out of my mind, if I'm reacting to you this way. Out loud she said, "I'm supposed to thank you for keeping your pants on?"

"You should." His lazy nod and the easy bulge of his heavy muscles as he negotiated another steep turn set off a whistling in her ears, a tightness inside her head. What was wrong with her? This was her nemesis! Her blood boiled near him with anger and frustration, nothing else. Maybe she was concussed. That would explain all those ridiculous reactions

"They stayed on only for your modesty's sake."

A belated realization hit her. "Oh, the tear gas…"

It must have dissolved in the rain, soaked his clothes. The longer they remained on him, the worse the injury he'd sustain, up to second-degree burns. Armed with the professional incentive, she took a closer look at his body and saw how flushed his polished bronze skin was. "Oh, for heaven's sake, you're erythematous! What ridiculous modesty. Take them off immediately."

"Trust me, I can't."

Did that mean he wasn't wearing—? "Oh!"

"*Oh* is right. La Clínica's near, anyway."

Recovering quickly, she asked, "Until then, shall I wash you down with a hypochlorite solution to neutralize the agent? Is it back there?"

"Hypochlorite is contra-indicated, Laura. It's good for other sorts of chemical contamination, but with CS or tear gas it only exacerbates the reaction."

"Oh!" She didn't know that. A good thing she wasn't ready with a bottle of the stuff. She bounced back with another suggestion. "What about another alkaline solution?"

"The one effective solution to relieve symptoms and hydrolyze the agent is a mix of sodium bicarbonate, sodium carbonate and benzalkonium chloride. Which I don't have! Another colossal oversight, going into a riot zone without it."

"You couldn't have known what to expect."

"I should have been prepared. I wasn't. If I suffer burns, it will teach me a good lesson."

"Aren't you being too melodramatic, suffering in punishment for a simple omission?"

"Says the woman who marched into the middle of a riot and nearly got trampled to death!"

"OK. *Touché.* But have you at least washed yourself off?"

"I did, even though that also makes it worse, acting like the rain did, since it wasn't a real hosing down. I only did it to decontaminate my skin just enough for when you slept on my lap."

Sensations and flashbacks burned their way up to her skin in a flush worse than his chemical burn. "You should've kept me awake."

"Why? You needed the rest."

"Well, I don't feel rested. I feel bent out of shape, permanently."

"And if I'd kept you awake, I would have been heartless and a nuisance."

"You could have left me sleeping in my seat with my seat belt on!"

"And have it pressing on the injuries it caused in the accident? My only other option was to throw you on the van's floor next to our patient. This archaic van doesn't have a secondary stretcher and—"

"OK, stop. You have it."

"Have what?"

"The last word."

Her answer was a long, sideways look that had her heart trying to hide in her gut. What was that in his eyes?

She didn't want to know.

She turned blind eyes away, searching for something to distract her. The sight of La Clínica De La Communidad hovering on the horizon wasn't a good choice.

Although her experience here had been a crushing disappointment on all fronts, the 'what if' factor was overpowering. She could have done a lot of good here. She could have found purpose and happiness. She'd found nothing but every sort of letdown.

Armando had bought this strategically situated, sprawling establishment from its owners after the collapse, giving them desperately needed cash for a dilapidated, money-pit mansion, many annexed buildings and the surrounding land. It had taken two years to renovate and equip it, to become a gravely needed and pioneering medical facility serving a hundred-mile radius, plus a far wider reach through its flying doctors service. Besides the usual medical services, La Clínica provided emergency surgical intervention to one quarter of the vast pampas region. And now through GAO's resources it was also reaching out to the wilderness of Patagonia and developing intensive care, research, education and rehabilitation facilities.

It was the dream of every doctor come true. Practicing medicine on their own terms, really making a difference, operating within a very elastic, responsive medium. A medical establishment based on the community's best interests and backed by its wholehearted support, not under governmental control, bound by decaying medical systems' undiscriminating rules or insurance's stifling restrictions.

Armando brought the car to a halt in the main building's emergency driveway, then turned to her. "Right. Back to bed until I say it's OK for you to leave it."

By the time his efficient emergency team had unloaded their patient, he was carrying her to a wheelchair, disregarding her protests.

Once inside, he ran to discard his contaminated clothes and apply first aid to his inflamed skin, leaving her in her GAO team's care, to suffer their deluge of questions. The doctor and two nurses who'd accompanied her from the US no longer knew what they were doing here and were constantly looking to her for answers and reassurance until she wanted to scream, *Stop asking me. I'm no longer in charge of anything. Ask the magnificent Dr. Salazar!*

She had to get away from here. Away from *him*. And if today had gone to plan she would have been packing now, not back at La Clínica and under his thumb.

She got up from the wheelchair, waving away assistance from her team. She'd walk back to her cell under her own steam.

On her way there, she couldn't help wincing again at the state of the building. The miserable veneer, the decaying columns and arches, the cracked walls, the stained, lusterless marble floors, all bore witness to Armando's refusal to restore anything that wasn't vital to the building's integrity and functionality. Hard to believe this place housed first-rate wards and state-of-the-art medical facilities. But it still needed so much more to realize its potential. So much more…

A nurse caught her eye, started to talk. Laura apologized for not stopping and kept her eyes glued to the main corridor's floor from then on, feeling everybody's curious glances prickling down her back. Suddenly, large sneakered feet planted themselves in her line of vision. No need to follow the endless denim-clad limbs up to know who it was.

"If you want to kill yourself, there are much quicker ways."

Armando didn't wait for a comeback, simply bent and carried her to the suite she'd been occupying since he'd let her out of Intensive Care. The moment he closed the door, she struggled out of his arms and onto her feet.

"I'm leaving, Salazar—now, not later." Her voice was unsteady, out of control. "And not only La Clínica but Argentina. That's why I was going to GAO's liaison office today. To arrange for my departure and replacement. I'll check into a hospital as soon as I arrive in the States—"

He cut off her agitated words. "You're not leaving. Not now and not when you're fully healed either!"

What? His next words made even less sense.

"You're staying here in Argentina, where I can make sure you and the baby are OK."

"What are you talking about? What baby?"

"Yours and Diego's. You do realize you're pregnant?"

CHAPTER THREE

"I'M *what*?"

A long, assessing glance answered Laura's shocked question. Then Armando shrugged. "So, you didn't realize. Anyway, you heard me, Laura. And you heard me correctly."

Hypoglycemia—she hadn't eaten since yesterday—that had to be it. Or auditory hallucinations. To be expected with all the sedatives and painkillers pumped into her system over the past week. Or maybe just a plain and simple breakdown.

She couldn't have heard him correctly!

"Don't look at me as if I've sprouted another head, Laura." A gentle grasp caught her hands in one of his, steered her to the bed. He lifted her up on it, then kneeled to take off her shoes. "I'll leave the rest of your clothes to Matilda. Now, *por favor*, Laura, let me check you. We'll talk about this later."

Matilda, the staff nurse he'd rung for, came bustling into the room. Cooing in Spanish, she expertly helped Laura off with her clothes and put her back into a hospital-issue gown. Armando had his back turned, busy reviewing her charts, writing down notes and directions for her continued care and medication schedule.

Once she was tucked up in bed, he came back to her. Her numbness deepened as he gently took her vitals, examined her, making sure her surgical wounds were intact. He deftly placed a cannula in her arm, unscrewed its cap and, dragging the mobile pole closer, placed the end of a saline bag's giving set on it. He set the drip, broke two ampules, injected one in the cannula's other outlet and one into the saline. Then he pressed the controls of a patient controlled analgesia pump in her hand

36

and attached an oximeter, to monitor her heartbeat and oxygen levels, to her other finger.

It was all happening to someone else.

That someone else was watching Armando about to close the door behind him after he'd dropped a bomb that had devastated her reality.

He'd said she was pregnant.

Pregnant!

"Armando!"

Armando froze, the temptation to swear a blue streak, to run, overwhelming.

This wasn't how he'd thought this would happen. Not that he'd given it much thought. He'd still been struggling to come to terms with it himself, and he'd hoped to have this confrontation only once he had. He'd had vague plans that they'd talk, about the baby and what next. He hadn't expected she'd push him into acting without thinking, hadn't expected she'd want to leave.

Not very bright since, come to think of it, it made sense she'd want to.

So. No use flaying himself over another bad call. *Her* bad calls were what mattered now. Judging by what she'd done today, her decision-making was obviously impaired. Only one priority existed. She was staying. He wasn't letting her go in her condition. And not with Diego's baby.

You just can't imagine seeing the last of her, Salazar, a candid voice in his head said. *Admit it.*

Oh, whatever! He just had to stop her in her tracks. And he surely had.

Not for long, though.

He dragged his feet back into the room, closed the door and leaned on it. "Laura, *por favor*, leave it till later."

Her laugh broke out, hysteria tingeing it. "When later? When I'm in labor?"

He stared at her, clutching the blanket, eyes wild, lips trembling. He didn't know what else to say.

"How could you possibly know I'm pregnant? When *I* sure as hell don't? When it's impossible?"

"It's not impossible. When you started deteriorating and I knew we had to operate, I had all sort of tests done. That's how I know."

"I didn't know pregnancy tests were routine before emergency ops!"

Shouldn't she be dulled by the sedative already—by everything else, for that matter? He shook his head and exhaled. "Normally, they aren't. But I asked for everything. Lab thought everything included a pregnancy test. It was a good thing, too. This way I picked category A medications and anesthetics that aren't harmful to fetal development."

"I still tell you it's impossible. I haven't—we haven't…" Her words trailed off, her angry agitation giving way to a look of supreme concentration. Followed by frightening pallor.

Laura felt her consciousness ebbing, then a wave of sickness rose, threatening to engulf her.

She'd fallen into Diego's arms at first, coming with all the building eagerness of their year-long online romance, of believing she'd finally found her soulmate. The one. Her rose-tinted glasses had been firmly in place and Diego's incredible good looks and concentrated charm had completed her dazzle. It hadn't taken long for reality to come into focus once more.

But they'd used protection and—and that *did* have a failure rate! As for the period she'd had recently, it *was* possible to have one at the beginning of a pregnancy…

Suddenly it was crucial to know. "How far along am I?"

"I'd say about eight weeks."

And since Diego had been dead one week, it had probably happened that last time. That time she'd known for sure she didn't want him any more. The time she'd told him it was over. Just over a month after they'd started their relationship. How ironic.

And how disastrous. An unwanted pregnancy, by an unwanted man. A dead man to boot!

But—but the tests could be wrong, maybe a mix-up. These things happened. *God—please, make it a mistake…*

The world receded. Armando blurred out of focus. Just before she lost sight of him, she thought, He's injected me with a sedative. A safe one for pregnant women, no doubt. How thoughtful…

Time stopped for Armando the moment Laura closed her eyes. He stared down at her sleeping her artificial sleep. An alien, disruptive sensation itched in his chest.

Three months since he'd first laid eyes on her. No way could he have predicted then that it would end like this. Diego dead, her pregnant, and him… What about him?

He was getting what he wanted at last—GAO's resources and connections. But GAO had been in Argentina for a long time, and they hadn't done much—until she'd come. She'd moved things, made things happen. Diego had said it had all been for him, to please him. That it was all her own personal clout and her family's.

He hadn't cared how he'd got help as long as he got it. That was, until he'd seen her.

Breathtaking had been the first thought that had filled his mind. *I want her* the second. The third *I can't have her*.

Diego had known. He'd looked his triumph into his eyes and bragged, "Isn't she something? And she's all mine."

So he'd resorted to being dismissive and remote. Then Diego had made it impossible to stay remote, so he'd stayed dismissive…

But he'd needed GAO, and this had meant more Laura, everywhere in his life. Then Diego had given him…details. More than he could stomach knowing. He'd told him how things had gone downhill, fast, how he'd no longer wanted her, how she'd clung. *That* hadn't sat right. He'd suspected Diego had been trying to save face. Laura didn't seem the type to cling to anyone.

Maybe he should have done something besides providing

an unwilling ear. If he had, maybe it wouldn't have ended up this way.

Yeah, sure. With his track record, they would have both fallen flat on their backs laughing if he'd preached relationship success.

Oh, he'd wanted their relationship to succeed, had he?

A token knock at the door cut through his mesmerized contemplation of Laura, bringing in Lucianna Perez, his godmother and head emergency nurse.

"Sorry, Armando, but there's been a huge fire in a high-rise housing complex in Rosario and medical services there are swamped and crying out for help. Most victims threw themselves out of windows and there are dozens of them. All multiple injuries besides the burns. Two firemen were injured, too. Since you're back, I thought you'd want to head the team going to the scene."

He nodded, snapping back to professional mode. But first… "Luci, get Matilda back in here. When her shift's over, her replacement takes her place. I want constant monitoring and minimum movement. Anything happens, no matter how minor and no matter where I am, report it immediately."

With a final look at Laura he ran out, putting on the fluorescent medical team yellow jacket Lucianna had handed him. "What's ready?"

Lucianna's answer was prompt—and regretful. "*El Bicho* is the only one left on the ground right now."

And was there any wonder why? His pilots avoided the archaic bucket of bolts so aptly called The Bug like the plague. Saddling him with it on his emergency flights was their way of protesting its existence on their meager fleet. As if he could afford to trash the monstrosity and had chosen not to! "And who's left behind?"

"Only Dr. Burnside's people."

Armando gritted his teeth. So the day had come when he was forced to take them on, rely on them. They'd been complaining of lack of occupation. Now they'd get it with a capital O.

With Laura spearheading them, they'd come believing that all that was needed to spread relief and stability was some cutting-edge medical equipment and a forced transfer to American medical protocols. They'd made no allowances for the incompatibility of an imported doctrine, or the ever-expanding shock waves that had fractured the very underpinning of society.

Laura's experience here so far had been with smiling politicians and eager media people. Today had been her first real dip into Argentinian reality—though he had to admit, she'd surprised him. Flabbergasted him more like. It took incredible guts and skill to do what she'd done back there. It took fearlessness. More, selflessness. Had he been that wrong about her?

Niggling shame uncoiled inside him. He fought it down. So he'd been wrong. He was man enough to admit it. But it didn't say she was qualified to run things here. If anything, it said she wasn't. She might be a far better doctor than he'd thought, a far better human being, but the fact still remained—that she was uninformed, out of her element. She needed him in charge until she learned, until she realized…she needed him…

His thoughts fogged with unbidden heat, then scattered at the sight of Laura's team running to meet him at the helipad.

The two blond men and the redheaded woman were watching him warily, but with a touch of defiance, too. He'd stepped hard on their toes, made them redundant. Now they'd be getting their baptism by literal fire. They'd all see if they could handle emergencies outside the luxurious protocols of American EMS services.

At the helicopter's door he turned to Lucianna who'd bustled after him, carrying fresh supplies. "Get Romero and Pablo to follow me to the location as soon as they hit ground from their emergencies, along with anyone who can be spared. Prepare ORs One through Four. We're low on blood, but get

Bank to give us all the O-neg they can. Send collectors over to our regular donors and beg for some more. Pay Luca and Estefan whatever they ask. It's out of my personal pocket so don't document it.''

He lowered his voice so Laura's team wouldn't hear him. ''I'd also feel better if you come with me this time. Just until we see how things pan out. This way I'll give you some more blood on the way, too.''

When she hesitated, he exhaled. ''*El Bicho* is safe, Luci. Noisy and bumpy and under-equipped but safe, OK?''

She nodded at once, trying to cover up her instinctive reaction. ''But you can't give me more blood!'' she objected. ''You just gave 850 mil a week ago, and that was a risk…''

''I eat like a horse. I've made it all up.''

''You know you couldn't have. And anyway I can't take blood from you while you're flying that—the helicopter!''

''Next to flying 'that—the helicopter' while fighting off a crazed nut on crack, it'll be a breeze. And it'll only take ten minutes.''

Lucianna tutted, her genial middle-aged face disapproving. But she knew it was useless arguing with him. She rushed back to get the necessary blood drawing and preserving equipment.

Once they lifted off, he presented her with his arm, obediently sipping the two bottles of fruit juice Laura's teammate, Nurse Susan Brent, held to his lips to compensate for the blood volume he was donating. He tried to concentrate on the coming crisis. And failed. His mind was with Laura.

What would he do with her?

What would *she* do?

She didn't want to open her eyes.

She had to. If only to escape the claustrophobic nightmares she was trapped in. But she'd open her eyes to a reality that was even worse for being inescapable. Yet taking refuge in oblivion, no matter how suffocating, wasn't an option any more. Her mind was already wide awake, her dilemma already in sharp focus and no way out in sight.

May as well get on with facing it all.

Laura sighed and opened her eyes. They immediately fell on Armando's silhouette, his exhausted pose in the armchair beside her bed unmistakable.

"That was some sigh."

His rasp shivered through her. Her internalized focus shifted with—concern? For *him*?

Rising to a sitting position in one brisk movement, she grimaced at her reaction, shaking off the softening. So he sustained an inhuman pace. It was one of the reasons she resented the hell out of him, wasn't it?

"And that was some imitation of life," she said. "What are you doing up? Trying to prove you're Superman again? Matilda said you've been on your feet between ER and OR for 72 hours. Since that was before I fell asleep—again—hours ago, you're into your fourth sleepless day!"

"You sure wake up sharp and ready with your math." He huffed a hoarse chuckle, rubbed both hands over his face and slumped further in the armchair. "I caught an hour here and there during that time." A silent heartbeat. "You've been crying."

"Matilda is a darling mother hen but an unprofessional busybody. She had no call reporting that to you."

"La Clínica isn't like your US metropolitan medical centers, Laura. We're close to each other here…"

"Too close, if you ask me!"

His eyes were barely visible in the faint indirect light, but she felt his gaze tightening. He went on, "And she was under strict instructions to report your very breath count."

"So she had to report its increase when I cried. And here you had me thinking she cared."

He sat forward in his chair, raked both hands again over his face and through his hair, expression still tight, unreadable. "She cares. We all do."

"Yes—yes, of course. I was trying for some comic relief..." Her words choked. She felt stupid. Worse, she felt tears rushing to her eyes again. How pathetic she must seem to everyone here. To him.

Suddenly it seemed all-important to know. "Does—does everyone...?" She couldn't say it, still couldn't believe it. She was *pregnant*!

Armando understood, ended her distress. "Only me and Berto at the lab. He won't tell anyone. That's one thing you don't have to worry about..." Armando let his words trail off, too, letting his head fall into his hands.

He really looked finished. And whether she felt sympathy for him or not, she was an extra burden he didn't need. She hadn't asked to be and it was his doing that she was, but, well, she wouldn't be any more. She had his word he'd take out her stitches and release her tomorrow. Then she'd return to that cursed villa Diego had saddled her with for a six-month period, start thinking how she'd put her messed-up life back together, making allowances for—for...

She was going to have a baby!

When she had no home, no money, no man for herself or a father for her baby!

Armando raised his head and even in the semi-darkness what she saw in his eyes was something totally unexpected—sympathy? Empathy? Whatever it was, it hurt, coming from him.

He heaved a deep sigh. "Did you think about...?" The eloquent gesture of his hands painted her plight.

An incredulous laugh almost choked her. "What do *you* think? But maybe you're right to ask. Thinking implies a rational mental process, not the panicking and obsessing I've been indulging in, considering my options..."

"Options?" His eyes emptied of empathy, if indeed it had been that. "What options? Adoption? Abortion?"

Those possibilities *had* entered her mind—only to exit the

other side as no options. But how dared he presume to have an opinion on this anyway? A judgmental one, too!

"And what if I am?" She swung her legs angrily off the bed. "What is it to you?"

He sprang to his feet, an impatient step bringing him looming over her, exuding power, tension crackling about him. He flicked an extra light on. Now his intensity was visible in every line of his features. His hand shot out. She tensed, only to be surprised by his extra-gentle, supportive grasp. He stunned her more when he talked, his awesome baritone devoid of rancor, almost soft again. "It is a lot to me. This is Diego's child."

How had that not occurred to her? Her baby shared Armando's blood. She should have realized what that would mean to a proud Argentinian who revered family ties above all else. Defiant indignation seeped out of her, and her rigid body slumped. "Those possibilities crossed my mind, OK? But, strange as it sounds, I actually want this baby."

It was his turn to be surprised. Heavy-lidded eyes widened. "You do?"

"Don't look so astonished! I didn't want this baby. Of course I didn't. But now it's real, growing inside me, I want it. If it sounds crazy…"

He waved away her words hastily. "No, no, it doesn't. It just never— I thought someone like you…"

Laura didn't answer that. Her expression did—and then some.

Armando sank his teeth into his tongue, sending a jolt of pain down his throat, along with the acrid taste of blood.

Fix this. You don't leave words like those hanging. He exhaled. "Laura, what I meant—"

An adamant hand stopped him. He breathed out again. He wasn't used to the taste of his foot in his mouth. He'd tasted it many times with her. Did wanting a woman and not being able to have her do this to a man? Turn him into a jerk?

She jumped off the bed in one lithe move, ignoring his protest and heading for the sofa on the other side of the room.

Even with all his over-protective pessimism, he could no longer keep her in bed. She *was* healed—would be walking out of La Clínica tomorrow. Out of Argentina.

The reminder was the kick in the gut he needed to try again. He followed her to the sofa, sat down heavily beside her. "I meant I thought you'd keep the baby but I didn't think you'd actually *want* it. It would only be human not to, considering the circumstances."

"So I'm human now? Not a cardboard cut-out from some shampoo ad or an inflatable character from a soap opera?"

Infierno! She'd heard *that*? How in hell had she? The stupid, sour words he'd hurled at Diego when too many glasses of wine had unleashed his frustration.

Was this his new role in life? Begging the woman's forgiveness?

Being at a loss was new to him. The disempowering feeling never assailed him, except with her. He hadn't learned how to handle it yet. He fell silent.

Laura watched him slump back in a flaccid pose, presenting her with his sharp-hewn profile, his heavy, arched eyebrows obscuring his eyes in a pitch-black frown. At least he wasn't denying having said those words. She opened her mouth. He spoke first, his voice that alarming lifeless drone again. "So you want the baby. Still want to leave Argentina?"

"Yes."

"Why?"

"Why stay? I came here to be with Diego…"

"And to work. Work is still here."

"Oh, really?" She pretended to search for it, up, down, around, behind him. "Where?"

He turned on her, his slanting eyes windows into an inferno. "All right. Let's have it out. Come on, give me what you got."

"Sure. Which eye do you want my left hook in?"

Black eyes widened, sweeping lashes flickered. An astonished rumble escaped his deep chest, followed by two rough chuckles in quick succession then unbridled guffawing.

It had been pseudo-smiles he'd given her so far—unsettling enough as they had been. But the sight and sound of his laughter…

Leash it in, Burnside. What's with the erratic heartbeat and the drooling?

This was her rival. Diego's cousin. He was off limits even for idle interest. So, he was an attractive man. Females collectively agreed on that. Fervently. Though attractive was no way to describe him. The one-of-a-kind looks, the overriding influence, the all-out maleness…

Oh, God! She was too vulnerable!

He sobered a bit. "Ah, Dr. Burnside. I've been discounting the evidence of my own ears. I had no idea you had a sense of humor. A wicked one, too!"

"And I had no idea you came ready with a laughter software package!" she threw back.

"You saying I'm a machine?"

"You saying I'm a bore?"

Laughter ebbed, only for his eyes to fill with more distressing things. Things she didn't care—didn't dare—put a name to. He leaned closer, bringing those things into sharp focus. "You putting words into my mouth?"

"Just interpreting the ones falling out of it. So far, there've been some real peaches."

"Your interpretation is way off. Far from finding you a bore, I…" The rest was caught between clamped teeth, his eyes narrowing on her, then swinging away. His inner debate was loud, but not clear. What was he thinking? What were the words he'd caught back? She was sure they weren't the ones he ended up saying.

"Listen, Laura, whatever grievances you have with me, and I'm sure there are plenty, give me that black eye and be done with it." He stopped again, his gaze sliding to the hands locked on her lap. "Though looking at your so-called left hook—'' her hand was suddenly in his, engulfed, a scrap of velvet in warm steel ''—I probably wouldn't feel a thing!''

Snatch your hand away, her mind ordered.

Her hand lay there in his, limply.

At least her tongue was still functioning. Just. ''Don't underestimate me,'' she gasped.

''And that's what I've been doing so far, haven't I?''

Let go of her hand, Salazar, reason urged. *This is the loaded American doctor who's playing at philanthropy, who thrives on media attention and online romances. Who's carrying your dead cousin's baby, for God's sake.*

Reason didn't even get a hearing. He pressed her hand harder. Then took it to his chest. Even through his shirt's rough fabric, the contact was so poignant, so long-craved, he groaned with it. And was that an answering moan on her lips?

''Armando…''

''Laura…''

He gestured for her to go ahead, she did the same and they both fell silent, staring at each other.

She snatched her hand away, jumping to her feet. He followed, spinning her round to face him. Her attempts to shake him off stalled when he caught her face in both hands, compelling her to look up at him.

''Would you stay if I promise not to bulldoze you any more?'' he urged.

''So you *do* know that's what you've been doing!'' Her hands dueled with him again. He only cupped her face tighter, awareness kicking higher in his blood. ''What I want to know is why? Just tell me *why*!''

''Because I believed you were not ready to handle the situation here,'' he said. ''Didn't understand the ramifications of local politics and social upheaval. Because I believed you'd do more damage than good with your semi-informed zeal and crew.'' Her eyes flared her resentment, and he decided to go for broke. ''And, hell, yes, I thought you were incompetent— and a flake to boot.''

Her eyes dissolved with a terrible emotion. *Dios!* Tears! Not angry but wounded, broken.

What had he done to her? What wouldn't he do to undo it? Would asking her forgiveness do this time? He had to try.

He kept her face enfolded in his grasp, her gaze trapped in his so she'd see his sincerity, feel his regret. "But I admit I was a prejudiced fool. And I'm not proud of it. I always took pride in thinking myself open-minded, in not pinning labels on people, in never going in with ready-made judgements. Four days ago in that riot, I learned how much of a fool I've been. Does this satisfy you, or do you want flesh? You're entitled to it."

She squeezed back a tear, threw him a condescending glance. "Keep your flesh. Not that you'd miss a pound or ten!"

Armando's startled laugh rang out. "You saying I'm fat?"

"Believe me, if you were even five pounds overweight, I would have rubbed your nose in it!" The tear escaped in spite of her concentrated effort to absorb it. It ran to her lips and her tongue came out to lap at the offending sign of vulnerability.

Let her go, Salazar. Before you do something insane!

Making a mental note to keep on wearing his toughest jeans around her, he said, his voice no longer under his control, "Will you stay, Laura? Let me make amends?"

"I can't stay, even if you promise to be my lapdog in this operation!"

"Let's not get too fanciful here..."

"Oh, yes. You only promised not to *bulldoze* me. Maybe you'll just flatten me a little less!"

"I promise I won't even wrinkle your clothes—if you're reasonable." His thumbs brushed her indignant mouth closed. Before his lips did. "Shush and tell me what you mean about you can't stay, even if I amend our working relationship to your satisfaction!"

"In case you haven't noticed, I'm pregnant—with an illegitimate child. The stigma of illegitimacy is still as strong as ever here. I'd be ridiculed professionally and despised socially. My child and I would be outcasts.''

''I admit American society is easier to blend into as a single mother. But wouldn't you, as a mother, exchange a few wagging tongues and censuring looks for your child's safety and comfort? You're rich and your family is influential, but no hired help money can buy will provide you with anything like La Clínica's extended family environment or its day-care facility, where you can get back to work right after you give birth and have your child safe only steps away.''

She gurgled a bitter, incredulous laugh. He wasn't sure what about. But she didn't answer, didn't pulverize his argument. He pressed his advantage.

''You can stay here and have a good life, give your child a good life. Despite the hardships, this is a great place to be. And if you're really serious about aid work, then this is a place that needs all the help it can get, a land of proud, passionate, hard-working people who've been knocked down from prosperity to destitution overnight. If it's truly your vocation, if you're like me, then there is nothing greater, nothing more fulfilling and reaffirming than giving such people, such a land a helping hand. Stay, Laura, do something that really counts, and bring up your child in the most beautiful place on earth.''

''That's a nice dream…''

''It doesn't have to be. It can be a reality. All you have to do is marry me.''

CHAPTER FOUR

"WHAT did you say?"

Yeah, what *had* he said?

He'd just asked Laura to marry him.

Marriage had never even featured in his life plans. And he was wide awake and as sharp as ever now.

So why had he?

His pager went off. OR was ready. Good, *great*. He wasn't. Not to explain himself. To either of them.

"Saved by the beeper, huh?" Laura sighed, her hands tightening on his forearms. It was only then he realized his hands were still around her face. And that he didn't want to remove them. He'd had his hands on her in so many ways before, shaking her hand, examining her, carrying her—operating on her. But now was the first real touch. He wanted to keep on touching her, to do far more than that, to do everything...

Her eyes flew to his when he resisted her, the translucent emerald becoming opaque, turning up his heat, and that of his fantasies. "Armando..."

His name on her lips—he'd never realized how erotic his name, any of his names, sounded until she'd said them. Every time she said them. Hearing her deep satin voice trembling with it now...he'd catch it in his lips, devour it. And her...

"Armando!" This wasn't a whisper now, it was a snarl. "You've taken your joke far enough. Now take your hands off me."

The pager beeped again, piercing the insanity gripping his senses. Saved by the beeper indeed. What he had in mind was too soon. Too rash. Too incendiary.

51

Back off. Get your hands to let her go. They wouldn't comply. They only glided from her face to her arms, in slow motion, holding her close when she attempted to pull back. An apology was ready on his tongue, but it too had a will of its own, saying what it wanted. "You'd better get used to my hands on you."

Before he succumbed and sealed her hanging-open mouth with his, before she recovered and gave him the slap he deserved, he stepped back. Tossing her a "Talk later" over his shoulder, he hurried to make an exit. Not fast enough, though. Her indignant *"Armando!"* aborted his escape.

He closed the door and turned, grimacing. *"Déjà vu,* Laura?"

"If you keep running away after dropping bombs, you should expect it. But this time I'm not calling you back to explain, but to tell you there won't be any 'talk later'. I'll get Jason to take out my stitches. And until I leave, I expect not to see you again!"

OK. So he'd messed up. Again. But there was no use trying to work it out gently now. It didn't bear risking. He walked back, scowled down at her. "Get this straight, Laura. There *will* be a 'talk later'. *I* will remove your stitches, and you're *not* leaving, so you'll see me *all* the time."

Arousal shot through him when a sharp intake of breath brought her luxurious breasts within an inch of his chest. As for the flare of animosity in her eloquent eyes…! Only one way to douse his fire—and hers. Two ways really. It was safer, all things considered, to go for the first way. "And if you have all that energy to argue with me, you're fit enough to work. Right now. Come and assist me in the OR."

The blaze dimmed in her eyes, only for cold resentment to replace it. How pathetic was it that it aroused him even more?

He sighed, resigned to his helpless reaction, and prompted, "Coming?"

Temptation crept over her face. He could almost feel her inner battle—needing to take a swing at him, wanting to take up his offer with equal urgency.

"Yes, Dr. Last Word!"

She marched out of the room ahead of him, and he followed her, his laugh ringing out again.

When was the last time he'd laughed like that? Never, that was when. Never quite like that…

"Welcome to OR Two, Laura!" Armando's voice rose over the music playing in the background. A smoochy tango number, the music alive, the singer's voice the embodiment of torrid Argentinian passion. As he was the senior surgeon, it must be playing at Armando's request. "Susan, Bank's getting ridiculous. I want that blood and platelets *now*."

Laura watched her teammate streak by her, giving her an excited grin on her way out. The energetic twenty-three-year old had been the one most out of her mind with boredom during their month of exile from work.

So Armando had started incorporating her team in his work, as promised. Not that that made her trust him. The man was too unpredictable, too ruthless, too used to getting his own way. She thought…

She didn't know *what* to think! He had apologized, had promised and he… He'd asked her to marry him, for crying out loud!

A tasteless joke that went out of control, she told herself. Probably under the effect of exhaustion and too much caffeine.

As she approached, she heard him humming along with the song and she almost swayed as his deep, melodious tones swept over her. He didn't look exhausted, or under the influence of anything now. He looked vital, alert. So what did it all mean? And what would it feel like to have that powerful body undulating against hers to that rhythm that had defined Argentina in her mind all her life?

Work, Laura. The cure for disturbing speculations and feelings. Work. At last.

She returned everybody's nods and murmurs of welcome. Her other teammate, Jason Leland, the anesthetist, even though a six-footer, stood four or five inches shorter than Armando. Constanza Ramirez, the general surgeon, an Argentinian beauty of around her age, was on Armando's right-hand side and, though taller than her, was still dwarfed by him. Arsenio Gonzalez, the orthopedic surgeon, was another Argentinian and Armando's best friend, and he looked like he'd be more at home on a pirate ship. His German wife Myra, the OR charge nurse, was his complete opposite, blonde and dainty.

Armando had left her in the scrubbing and gowning-up area, having concluded his own preparations much faster than her. He just had to be an over-achiever in everything, didn't he? Then he made it even worse.

"Myra, bring Laura a high chair next to Constanza," he said.

She'd expected a step, since the table was adjusted to his height, and she wouldn't have seen anything from her disadvantaged, foot-shorter position. But a high chair?

"I've already been fed, thank you, Armando!" Her sarcastic streak had resurfaced and was out of control. But why should she control it? After what he'd said and done to her, he deserved anything she tossed at him.

After a second's silence, they all burst out laughing at her barb, only Myra with her weak colloquial English not getting it.

While the other three explained it to Myra, Armando whispered, for Laura's ears only, when she passed him, "I should have known, since you don't have your bib on!"

So he could give as good and better than he got. Who would have thought it? And she *wouldn't* smile.

Eyeing the chair now beside Constanza, Laura shot Armando a speaking glance. The challenging one he shot back set off ridiculous mini-fireworks inside her.

"Don't glare at me like that, Laura." Not that he sounded at all concerned that she was. "You're sitting this one out."

"Why? You think I'll collapse under the weight of a scalpel?"

"Humor me. Let's be safe rather than sorry, hmm?"

"Just who's going to be safe and who's going to be sorry?"

"You're not missing anything, Laura," Constanza intervened. "This is a boring appendectomy."

"Appendectomy!" Laura did a double-take, starting at the man's mangled left leg.

Arsenio shook his head. "I still can't believe how it happened myself. Mr. Perez here had such a sudden, powerful attack of colic that he jumped in front of the first cab he saw to bring him here. The cab gave him that lovely tibia-fibula compound fracture."

"And brought him here," Jason added.

"It turned out he did have acute appendicitis," Constanza said. "With impending perforation. So it was a good thing he panicked."

"Ouch. Poor man." Laura grimaced.

"Let's begin, people," Armando said the second Susan came back with the blood and blood constituents. "And you, Laura, *sit*! If you're still awake after we're finished, I might consider letting you assist me in the next op."

"What next op? You have an emergency op *scheduled*?"

They all chuckled again at her frustration and Constanza mock-groaned, "Have mercy, Laura. Don't be so eager to work or you'll bring on us another week like the one we've just had!"

Laura exhaled in resignation, sat in her elevated position and watched them going through the practiced procedures, each pair working together in one area of the patient's body. They were all very good, but she had to admit— Armando was more. The best she'd ever seen. Almost supernatural in speed and precision. And right now it made her angrier than ever with him.

He finally looked up and met her infuriated eyes directly. She dragged her mask down and mouthed, "You tricked me!"

And he only winked at her!

Her heart stopped—then burst out in a stumbling gallop.

What was going on? *This* was Armando Salazar? The man who'd treated her like a sexless nuisance at work and an inanimate object outside it? There was nothing sexless about that wink. Or about his every look and touch back in her room. Was he *really* coming on to her? Was the seasoned ladies' man reverting to form around her now he no longer considered her off limits?

She sought his eyes for an answer. Caught them as Mr. Perez was wheeled to Recovery and Armando was directing Jason about their patient's post-operative care. No flirtation there now. In fact, he looked fed up. With her? Or with himself for letting that suggestive wink slip? Still, his dark scowl had an even worse effect. Was that how every woman he focused on felt? Mesmerized, helpless—out of control?

Get busy! Useful actions, not dim-witted reactions.

But there was nothing to get busy with.

Just in time to save her sanity, Constanza said, "Since you're still wide awake, you deserve some good news. There *is* a second emergency and scheduled operation. Still, it's up to Armando who gets to assist."

Laura smiled into the woman's warm brown eyes, the last thing she felt like doing. Constanza was fluttering her long lashes at Armando, while he looked from one to the other like a sultan choosing a harem member for the night. Then he shook his head.

"Go crash, Constanza," Armando said. "If you don't, instruments will start disappearing into our patients' abdomens."

Constanza heartily chuckled as she walked out, just as Jason returned.

"What's the new joke?" Jason asked eagerly.

Laura gave a theatrical sigh. "It's priceless. Our fearless leader thinks a woman is a hazard whether she's been awake or asleep too long. Hate to hear his views on a woman with PMS."

Armando watched Jason's blue eyes gleam with appreciation and…discovery? Was he, too, seeing Laura as if for the first time? It seemed so.

Jason kept chuckling at anything Laura said, until Armando felt like lashing out at him about how silly it was for a grown man to giggle. Not that Jason was giggling. There was nothing silly or effeminate about either his looks or attitude. And Laura wasn't throwing visual daggers at *him*. On the contrary…

What was wrong with him? He'd blatantly flirted with her, asked her to marry him, almost kissed her—wanted to do much, much more. And Diego had been dead only twelve days!

OK, so it had been over between them long before he died. But the fact remained that she was carrying Diego's baby, and he couldn't still want her—couldn't be feeling like breaking in half any man who came near her.

So Jason liked Laura. Why not? Let him like her. Let her like Jason. She certainly didn't like *him*. Another fact remained. She needed help, needed a man—so maybe Jason…

No! No way!

If she needed a man, that man would be *him*.

"…this *scheduled* emergency case?"

He caught the end of her question as she scrubbed again next to him. What had she said? Did she have to stand so close?

But she wasn't close, *he* was too inflamed. *Concentrate—cool it,* he ordered his rampaging senses. The operation was in minutes. He'd better locate the switch to his professionalism.

"A condensed case history, since you're so interested," he said, his eyes straying to hers no matter how he tried to keep them away. "Señora Ascuncion Villa, 74 years old, admitted via ER three hours ago complaining of shortness of breath, nausea, vomiting and abdominal pain after meals that has become acutely unbearable. Chest X-rays showed a raised left hemidiaphragm, healed rib fractures with a collapsed left lung."

"No history of trauma?" Laura's wide eyes became huge with interest. It was a good thing he could do none of the outrageous things rushing through his fantasies with his OR staff wheeling in their patient past them.

"She insisted so." He held the swinging door open with his elbow for her to re-enter the OR ahead of him, the almost-brush of her body against him causing another bolt of torment. "Clinical evidence says otherwise." His voice was tight as they took their places again.

"You think it may be a case of elder abuse? That she's covering it up?"

"The possibility jumped into my mind, too, since she's living with her son and his wife. But if it is, then it's the first time it happened. I had total body X-rays done and there are no signs of any healed fractures."

"So, did you find out how she sustained the injury?"

"After extensive questioning, she admitted to having slipped in the bathroom five months ago. The emergency department of another hospital discharged her after an overnight stay with analgesia. They told her the X-ray they took at the time showed nothing out of the ordinary."

Laura raised her winged eyebrows. "She had those with her?"

"Yes, very hazy, minus the report."

"Done CT scans?"

Why was she asking when she already knew? She was the one who had got him the new computerized tomography machine. GAO personnel had only finished installing it hours ago. She knew there was a huge backlog of priority cases. "Yes, but since it could be hours until Radiology get their act together and produce printouts and reports, I elected not to wait for them."

"So you scheduled her for emergency operation, based on your diagnosis and a non-conclusive set of X-rays?"

"*Ciertamente*. Clinical evidence was solid, and the ridiculed X-rays are enough in my book. CT scans are just to be extra sure and for documentation."

"I know." Green eyes danced. She'd got him to defend his decisions again. And relished it.

His heart hammered. The sheer…fun of the woman!

But if this was the real her, what had been wrong between her and Diego that she'd been so put out all the time?

His attention snapped back to her exchange with Jason.

"Why is she already out?" she asked.

"I deeply sedated her when I gave her her pre-anesthetic medications," Jason said. "She was very agitated, wanting to get up and go home."

Armando nodded. "She kept saying she'd never even taken aspirin before. Pleaded with me to let her go. She was really freaking out at the idea of being put to sleep, being cut open."

At that moment Myra came in with Señora Ascuncion's CT scans. Laura whistled. "Radiology comes through!"

Armando took a look at them before passing them to her.

She summed up the findings thoughtfully. "Hmm. Everything you said, plus the stomach in the left thoracic cavity."

Armando clapped his hands. "OK, let's go in and put everything back where it belongs."

The team gathered round, Jason starting their patient's deep anesthesia and placing her breathing support and monitors. Then Laura and Myra quickly prepped her trunk with packs soaked in antiseptic skin solution and draped her securely for maximum warmth, leaving only the operating field exposed.

Armando watched the sure practiced movements of Laura's dainty, gloved hands. Would she be as deft with a scalpel? Had her six-year residency been well spent or had she gotten preferential treatment in that surgery department her father had founded? He was about to find out.

Jason cleared his throat. "Arterial line in, Armando. Her vitals are iffy."

"OK. Laura, you know what this means. Let's race."

He handed her the scalpel and she immediately performed a midline incision in one sure stroke. Good. *Very* good. He followed through, widening the gap and placing self-retaining retractors, opening the operating field and keeping it open.

"Feel that?" He removed his hands so she could put hers in. She raised her eyes to his.

"What a squeeze. The diaphragmatic laceration is just about ten centimetres and approximately two-thirds of the stomach and the spleen have compressed through it into the chest. No wonder she was vomiting and in pain."

"And she put up with it for five months. OK, Laura, extend the laceration laterally."

He watched as Laura widened the diaphragmatic defect to double its original size, returning the stomach and spleen to their original positions with complete economy of movement. This was a surgeon who knew what she was doing.

"Whew," she said. "Will you look at that band-like constriction in her stomach? That diaphragmatic defect was like a vise around it!"

"People, you want to hurry!" Jason warned again.

"We have five more minutes. Wash out the chest, Laura."

She did that while Myra swabbed and suctioned. "Nylon sutures, Myra. Two strands. One for me and one for Laura," he said. "Laura, you close the diaphragm, continuous sutures. I'll place two stay sutures on either side of the laceration, so the diaphragm will be tented downwards to aid closure."

Laura nodded and in under two minutes had completed her meticulous task.

"Want to close her up?" He quirked an eyebrow at her.

She nodded eagerly and immediately began closing the layers of peritoneum, muscles, subcutaneous fat and tissue. As she worked on the final layer, the skin, he nodded to Jason. "Bring her out. How is she?"

"She'll be fine—now!" Jason exhaled. "It's as if she knows it's over. I felt as if she was fighting us, scaring us into letting her go."

"She probably was. I get the feeling I'm not going to get any thanks from her when she wakes up."

Laura shook her head. "When she wakes up nausea- and pain-free, she'll thank you."

"You think so?" He gave her a long, considering look and watched the elation of surgery well performed ebb from her eyes, the slow burn of challenging antagonism he was getting used to replacing it. "I remember another recent laparotomy patient. I've been on top of her hate list ever since I saved her life!"

"Will you marry me?"

"Will you stop it?"

Armando had put his head around her door just as she placed the final pin in her hair. And just as she was turning to him, an apology on her lips, he had to say *that*!

Now, how could she be anything but a shrew to him?

Ignore him, she told herself. *Or joke it away. Remember, whatever else he's done, he has saved you—twice. Just say thank you and get out of here!*

But if the impassive Armando had been hard to ignore, that bedeviling one was impossible to.

"Whose stitches are coming out?" He advanced on her with a mischievous grin, scissors snapping in the air.

"Who woke up in a chirpy mood today?"

"I always wake up chirpy."

"Oh, sorry, I got the wrong man, then. You just look like an ogre I know—Armando Salazar. Maybe you've met him?"

He threw his head back and laughed. "Sure I did, in the bathroom just ten minutes ago. Great guy."

No kidding! And it was no joking matter either, the way her heart was ricocheting inside her. "This is very disturbing, you know. A real case of Dr. Jekyll and Mr. Hyde."

"Can't a man have a good day once in a while?" He didn't give her a chance to say anything, dragging her to face him, removing her dressings. "Now, let me see…"

For the next five minutes, he carefully snipped the stitches and pulled them out. Then finally he drew away and gave her a critical look.

"What?" she snapped.

He turned her by her shoulders to face the mirror. "See for yourself!"

She gasped, her eyes filling.

Her face! She'd expected—expected far worse!

Stepping closer to the mirror, she ran tentative fingers along her faint healing scars. They'd fade away even more with time. One ran from the corner of her eyebrow to her ear. Another along her hairline. Another in the laughter crease in her cheek. And a last one along her jaw. And they were all negligible.

She turned to him. "Oh, Armando!"

"Happy, Laura?" His voice was black molasses and she—she...

She swung her fist as hard as she could and caught him solidly in his arm. "You creep," she cried. "You tricked me again. You made me think I'd be the new Frankenstein's bride. I was scared to even peek!"

He rubbed his arm, his grin widening. "I had to scare you into staying put, so you'd heal perfectly. But this is even beyond my best hopes. That skin of yours—you must have one of the lowest scarring tendencies on record. Congratulations, *querida*."

Querida? Oh, how could he?

She turned away from him, freeing her hair, brushing it with shaking hands, letting her long bang cover the most visible scar.

"Now it's time for that 'talk later', Laura." He took the brush out of her hand, ran his fingers through the thick fall of her hair. She was sure her lungs would burst with the next breath. "There's not much to say, though. Marry me. Right away."

She snatched her eyes away, stumbled a step backwards. "This is ridiculous, Armando. You're being irrational. And heaven knows, with everything that's happened to me in the last months, with what's coming, I must be, too. Let's just forget the last twenty-four hours happened, OK?"

"Can *you* forget them?" He sounded serious again, his face once more the impassive, beautiful mask she'd been used to.

"I may not forget them, but it's only sensible to overlook them. You're not yourself..."

"And you know everything about me, Laura?"

"I know nothing about you."

"You know enough."

"Enough for what? You can't mean..."

"I can and I do. Every word."

She turned away, found him somehow in front of her

again, filling her eyes, her awareness. He glided over the remaining step between them, put a finger beneath her chin and raised her face. His black eyes were a dizzying mix of intensity and enticement. Her heart stuttered, then stopped when he said, "*Venida*, Laura. Let me take you home. My home. *Your* future home."

Armando's Spanish-style villa zoomed closer amidst its fenced acres. The cattle and crops of Armando's father's time were long gone, and wilderness had reclaimed the land. She'd heard the stories and mourned the waste.

Jolted out of her dark reverie by the jerking of Armando's old four-by-four's poorly tuned engine, she realized he'd already stopped in front of his porch, jumped out of the car, opened her door and was extending a hand to her. Hers unthinkingly answered, letting him hand her down, draw her close. She gazed up at him, lost, the need to take refuge in his embrace swamping her.

Every time she'd come here, she'd ached. Every brick and brushstroke around the place appealed to her tastes and dreams. Diego had told her they'd build a home like that. A house reminiscent of an old world hacienda, with tile roof and adobe-style bricks, in the middle of land like this. But he'd bragged that that would be where the resemblance ended. Their villa would be elegant and sparkling, not like this crumbling mammoth which hadn't seen a fresh coat of paint in over a decade.

He simply hadn't understood. It was the place's very age, the passionate memories permeating it that made it almost alive, enfolding. Nothing new and polished would ever compare.

Something rumbled in Armando's powerful chest when she remained transfixed. His arm around her shoulders urged her onwards and up the steps to his vine-entwined, covered patio and through the double doors leading from the entry into the columned foyer. And as always, the house breathed its happy history into her, of family love and laughter and loyalty—everything she'd been deprived of.

Caustic memories of an angry child who'd had no one to turn to ate into her once more. The twelve-foot-high sloping ceiling of the open-plan living area choked her, the lingering echoes of lively family gatherings underlining the silent isolation of her life.

Her glance strayed towards the spiral stairs leading to the first floor. Diego had shown her around once. She remembered only the master bedroom, its bathroom with the raised tub nestling under a skylight...

"I know the place hasn't aged gracefully." Armando's quiet words broke into her forbidden thoughts. Heat rushed to her head, cascaded down her body.

"You're not serious!"

Armando sighed in relief. At last she'd said something. Ever since he'd dragged her out of La Clínica, she'd been looking at him as if he were a dangerous lunatic—worse, as if he'd just crawled out of the nearest sewer.

"What does that apply to? My marriage proposal, or the villa not aging gracefully?"

"This place is—*gorgeous*. No matter what condition it's in."

"That's half the battle, then. You like the house enough to live in it. Now all that's left is for you to like its owner enough to marry him."

"Armando, please stop. You can't be in your right mind. You can't be serious."

He looked heavenward, found nothing of help there and closed his eyes, begging for patience, for the right way to handle this.

"I am serious. Dead serious," he finally said.

"But why?"

Why, indeed? That was the hardest question of his life. Why was he asking her to marry him? He had reasons why not to. And only two reasons why he should. He wanted her—*wanted* her! And he wanted the baby.

Were those good enough reasons to drive a man to marriage?

He groaned. *Drive* a man to marriage? Like driving him insane or to his ruin? He'd better not let something like that slip out loud. She was resistant and skeptical enough already. And he wanted her to say yes, didn't he?

Well, didn't he? Or was he just offering and hoping she'd turn him down?

He looked at her again, standing there in the middle of his family home, empty now but the place of his most cherished memories, her lithe figure and bright spirit making the same old surroundings new, exciting, a setting for making even better memories, for bringing fantasies to life…

No. He wanted her to say yes. Couldn't wait for her to. Say it over and over. Cry it out to him, while he…

He buried hands that itched to reach for her in his pockets and immediately removed them when he realized it only drew attention to his…state. He sat down on one of the beige and brick faded Moroccan-style sofas, drew a concealing cushion onto his lap and patted the space beside him. That only won him a firm shake of her head, undulating all that spun night around her elfin face, tumbling it over her high, generous breasts.

His hands started to burn and any sitting position became painful. He needed her eyes off him. Talk. Talking would distract him, her. She'd asked him something, hadn't she?

Oh, yes. "Why?" He huffed an incredulous laugh. "You're the most baffling woman I've even known. Here I am, asking a woman for the first time in my life to marry me, and she all but recommends I undergo psychiatric evaluation!"

"If the shoe fits!"

"I assure you, I, Armando Salazar, am of sound mind and body, and I *am* asking you to marry me."

"Why do you want to get married at all? Aren't you perfectly happy being a playb—being free?"

"Now, that's another new twist. I'm not being arrogant here, but every woman I've ever met has tried to advertise marriage to me as the only reason for living!"

"And, of course, any of them would fall to her knees in thanks if you so much as smiled at her."

"But not you, eh? Maybe that's why I want to marry you."

"Armando!"

"All right. Why I want to get married. I'm pushing forty—"

"You are?"

"I'll be thirty-nine in a couple of months. My mother would love me to get married—"

"Your mother's alive?"

"No, but, trust me, she's up there waiting for the day. Now stop interrupting me. 'Being a playb—being free', as you so eloquently put it, especially in this country, is getting monotonous and too much work for ultimately nothing. I expect I will buckle under social demands and get married sooner or later, so why not now? The usual mid-life crisis, really."

"You expect me to believe that?"

Armand sighed. What did it take to satisfy her? The truth? He doubted it. But what would Laura do if he told her he hadn't slept one solid night since he'd laid eyes on her? That he hadn't known such violent sexual attraction possible, that it made him wonder if it *was* a symptom of a breakdown of some sort? That all he could think of when he had a moment to himself was how it would feel to have his body buried in hers, his senses full of her taste and his head full of her cries of pleasure?

She'd probably call him a pervert and run screaming.

Exaggerate, he told himself, *make fun of it. Throw her off track, alleviate her suspicions.* He smiled his easiest smile. "I no longer know what to expect from you. What *would* you believe? That I'm madly in love with you and will go on a hunger strike and fade away if you don't marry me?"

She laughed and his fist went to his chest, pressed the ache there. That laugh! Good thing she hadn't been in the habit of laughing before. But if she was going to be, and it did this to him every time, he was looking at a drastically shortened life span.

"You're funny, Armando." She wiped tears of laughter, her solitary dimple winking at him. He pressed his chest harder. "I would have never believed it, but you are. So, let's say I buy the reasons why you decided to take the plunge, the really tough question remains: Why me? That's more like walking the plank!"

"Want an alphabetized list? You'd make an Attractive wife, there's a Baby to consider, we're Compatible, we're both Doctors…"

"Hey, hey, excuse me! The only one who has to consider the baby is me! And we're compatible? How so?"

"How are any man and woman compatible?"

Her velvet cheeks turned peach, her delicate rosy lips pursed. He went on before he dragged her onto his lap and unpursed them for her. "We're compatible, age-wise, career-wise and, as hard as it is for both of us to believe, it seems temperament-wise, too." Better not stress the area he believed them most compatible in. She wasn't ready for that yet.

She looked at him for a long, long moment, her eyes losing their gleam, a pained expression invading them, tightening her open face. He wasn't ready for the pain her pain caused him.

He found himself on his feet, reaching out to her. She warded him off with an outstretched hand.

"I understand now." Her voice was ragged, muffled.

"Sorry for being so dense. You *pity* me. Along with feeling a crazy sense of duty."

"You're wrong…"

Her rising voice drowned out the rest of his words. "Those are no reasons to marry anyone, it would only lead to misery. And don't you *dare* pity me. I'm not some helpless girl. Even if I stay here, I will stand up to whatever social censure is thrown at me. I don't need a man to protect me. I've been on my own almost all my life and I'll be fine on my own again."

"But you *won't* be on your own." This time he also raised his voice. He was losing her, and he had to play all his cards, hard, keep her from slipping away. "A baby changes everything. A baby needs a father as much as a mother. And you may think you want to be on your own now, but you're young and one day you *will* want a man— a husband, at least a lover. What other man but me would you trust to love your child as his own?"

She winced, her eyes reddening, filling then overflowing. "That's hitting below the belt, Armando!"

"That's just being frank."

"Haven't you thought what it would be like for you? I wasn't even officially engaged to Diego. What would people say about you if you married someone like me?"

"Never worry about me, Laura. I took care of ruining my own reputation long ago. It's your reputations, yours and the baby's, that I care about."

"Whose reputations? The loose woman's, who'd marry her lover's cousin before he's cold in his grave, and the illegitimate child's?"

Put that way, it didn't sound pretty. But it wasn't how it really was.

Then it hit him. *Yes!* That would take care of everything.

He caught her by the shoulders and looked into her drowned eyes, exerting all his will-power on her. "Listen to me, Laura. You and Diego were finished before he died. If anyone asks, and I'd like to see who'll dare, you say you split up because of me. We'll get married at once and say the baby's mine!''

CHAPTER FIVE

"...I DO."

Armando closed his eyes, letting Laura's fervent words roll over him, and prayed for patience.

God wasn't handing out any today.

He erupted. "Is it that much to ask, for you to actually consider something sane for a change?"

"Sane according to you is putting my feet up until the baby's born, preferably for ever, and getting out of your hair," she retorted, fists curled on curvaceous hips, eyes explicit with the need to get physical with him. If only it was in the way he craved. "You're already welshing on your promises, and I repeat, in case you haven't heard me—I won't let you put me on the sidelines again. I'll be damned if I do!"

"Even though I think I'll be damned if I *don't*, I repeat too: I'm not trying to put you anywhere." *Except in my bed,* the ever-aroused voice inside him said. He squashed it silent. "I'm only suggesting that until the pregnancy is stable, you shouldn't pick the most physically demanding assignments and cry fraud and murder when I say you shouldn't be on them!"

"Say? You don't say! You just went ahead and excluded me—again. And what was so physically demanding about flying to negotiate with the Brazilian medical supplies distributors and to release the shipments GAO sent over to Bahía Blanca? In La Clínica you may be lord of all you survey, but these were procedures I started, and you had *no* right to finalize them without my approval and presence. I'm GAO's authorized medical co-ordinator—"

He cut through her tirade. "And I'm GAO's local administrative consultant and executive. And you think a round trip

71

across the continent and back in one day isn't demanding? Next to violently out-of-control riots, you mean?''

Laura continued as if he hadn't said anything. "So, since you've covered essential medicines and basic supplies needs in two hospitals each in Mendoza, San Juan and Mar Del Plata for the next six months, *you* can put your feet up while I go to the Jujuy and Salta provinces.''

"But these are the furthest north and a brutal heatwave is hitting them.''

"I'm not made of cotton candy, I won't melt!''

Whatever he was going to say caught in a throat suddenly too tight to let another word out.

No. He shouldn't. He *really* shouldn't. She hadn't said yes yet and he shouldn't give her more reasons to say no.

But maybe you should, that feverish voice whispered its heated suggestion again. *Maybe it's the only way you'll get that yes.*

They were outside La Clínica's main entrance, out in the open, with workers, colleagues and patients buzzing around, casting openly amused glances at their boisterous debate. He may as well give them something worth watching.

He closed the space between them, heard her yelp as she stumbled backwards only to find a column behind her. He smiled. *Got her.*

Bearing down on her, he pressed her, her softness cushioning his hardness, his hands securing her head, tilting up her stunned face. "So you won't melt, huh? Let's see…'' He breathed out the words then breathed her in. Her eyes turned dark olive with shock and he hesitated.

Just do it.

He did. Took her lips. And was electrified. Literally. A surge of static electricity crackled between their lips, sending his head jerking backwards.

For a suspended moment, he stared at her, watched her staring back at him, silent admissions and equal awareness filling her eyes.

Then just as suddenly polarity reversed. He pressed back on her, helpless now, no longer the instigator. He sank his mouth in hers, needing more of her with each restless glide against her lips, striving for a deeper taste, a fuller merging. Then she opened to his invading tongue and flooded his system like an aphrodisiac overdose.

He'd dreamed, when he shouldn't have. He'd known—but could have never known it could be like that...

Sounds of amusement infiltrated his fogged awareness, the laughter and cat calls infuriating him far less than his inability to sever the connection. And he'd thought he could handle it, put out the fire when he chose.

Stupid, the voice in his head sniggered. *She makes you stupid. She makes you someone you don't know, can't control.*

No. He would exercise his vaunted control—pretend to, at least.

He willed his locked muscles to neutral, extricating himself, standing a separate being again. At least he hadn't been alone in losing it. She'd been just as lost—hadn't she?

At the first tug of separation, Laura's senses shrieked. He couldn't just pull back!

He did. She stared into obsidian eyes as he took her breath away with him. He looked the same. How dared he look the same?

But, no, he wasn't the same. Harsher, more elusive, more—more... Surely he hadn't always been that beautiful? And was that a touch of triumph, too?

It figured. She'd melted all right. Run like water through his fingers. With just a kiss—here, with the world watching.

Could she possibly hate him any more?

Fury at him—and at herself—activated her muted voice. "Did that show have a point, Salazar, besides preventing me from winning the argument, shutting me up in the most chauvinistic, barbaric, *outdated* way possible?"

His regal head inclined, one shoulder rising in a careless

shrug, stretching the khaki shirt across his mighty torso. Blood fizzed in her ears.

Sex. That was all it was. And was there any wonder why? She was vulnerable, scared and frustrated. So frustrated—all her life. He was an over-endowed brute. End of story. And she really would be damned if she let him—let him... He was reaching for her again. No!

He caught her. ''We've given the good people here more than enough free entertainment.'' He dropped the urging into her ear as he propelled her to his office. ''Let's continue the battle in private.''

In private? No way. Being alone with him warped her mind. After that kiss, what it revealed about him, about her, 'in private' was a catastrophe in the making. And he thought she'd marry him? There were quicker highways to annihilation!

''The battle's over,'' she hissed, suppressing her shivering. ''From now on we're splitting chores, and that's that!''

Armando stopped, took his hand off her arm, faced her, the need to bulldoze her emblazoned on his hard features. Then he shook his head, dropped his eyes and examined his feet for a long, absorbed moment.

She held her breath. What would he say?

''Lay off hard work, just until your first trimester is over...'' Her automatic forceful refusal slammed to the back of her throat when he closed his eyes and groaned, a tortured sound that shook her. ''Please, Laura, just give me this little scrap of peace of mind. I *need* it.''

The world carried on, the hectic pace of work in La Clínica sweeping around them, while they stood in stasis.

Those moments of suspended animation and silent communication were getting too weird. Was she having a long overdue breakdown after all?

Had she really heard him begging her, admitting to a need?

This could be interesting. Time for some plain talking. Oh, yes!

In a second it was her fingers that were digging into his

iron-hard arm, her other hand flat on his back as she propelled him to his office. He looked stunned, and she almost laughed. She did chuckle. It felt fabulous, seeing him in less than total control.

Passing through his waiting room, she nodded to his two assistants, both women, of course, and clearly besotted, asked for coffee for two and pushed him into his spacious, shabby office-examination room.

He turned to her the moment she closed the door, arms spread, his expression completing the portrait of his bafflement.

"Did I miss something or will this start making sense soon?" he said.

"I came here with a mission mapped out, Armando—"

"So, it's *Armando* again!"

"And this mission was two-fold—a lobbying part and a hands-on part. I admit for a while there at the beginning I was overwhelmed—for a combination of reasons—and wasted a long time on the very minimum of tasks required, falling way behind schedule. That was probably why GAO smothered you in kisses and accepted your proposal for an existing and solid base of operation in Argentina, since they thought I wouldn't prove effective."

Armando didn't have a clue where this was leading, but his acute sense of fairness stabbed him. He had to say something.

"If they thought so, they were both unfair and wrong. I've watched them, and other aid operations, muddle their way here with short-term and futile measures. You've been here— what?" *Ninety-eight days.* He pretended to make an estimate. "Two, three months? And how much of that time was actually on the job? You may not have done a lot, but you've certainly done a lot more than any of the other medical co-ordinators I've seen. You've put in motion the most effective campaign to get authorities to tackle access to health care in the region."

"Maybe it's because I pushed GAO's proposals at a time of relative stability, with the elected government in place for more than the usual few weeks in the merry-go-round of the last four years!''

He waved away her reasoning. ''Whatever the reason, I've been having the most help from authorities ever since you arrived, even before signing up with GAO, when before I only had prohibitions and hurdles. The current situation is still brutal and untenable, but it has nothing to do with any individual aid operation's success or failure.''

''But the logistics I had coming in said there should be a visible change in the places we targeted within the first two months. I certainly hadn't seen them, and it was why I believed it was me who'd been doing a lousy job. It was really why I didn't fight you tooth and nail, and let you walk all over me.''

He winced at her even-voiced description of his treatment of her. Then he frowned as he remembered the smartass logisticians he'd talked to, the ones he'd delightedly and permanently bent out of shape. Which one had been responsible for her miscalculations and misplaced expectations?

Savage adrenaline coursed in his system. ''What I told the geniuses responsible for your charted course and expected figures isn't for ladylike ears. There was no way any change could have been felt in that time frame. You were targeting public health system establishments, and those used to provide care for twenty to thirty per cent of the population. Today, they're trying to tend to up to sixty or seventy per cent. Hospitals have been working beyond their capacity for years, with the demand rising, leaving them without even basic supplies. The shortage worsened when people covered by private medical insurance were excluded from them overnight, and became completely dependent on the crumbling public health system. If the Argentina Project's logisticians expected GAO to put even one major public hospital on track in two months, I guess I owe them another, more explicit phone call.

''As any moron could tell, *this*...'' he made an angry, encompassing gesture ''...won't be resolved in a year, or a decade, maybe not even in our lifetimes. That's why we need places like La Clínica, non-profit centers outside both private and public health structures; why we need organizations like GAO, provided they're coming in with realistic plans and expectations. We need those, the more the better, the more united the better. But it certainly hasn't been *your* fault it's taking for ever for a difference to be felt in a crisis that has left ten million people without access to drugs or health care!''

His agitation as he relived his country's plight gave way to something else. A feeling of having stumbled into a trap, but not knowing what it was—yet. Silence rang with his impassioned words. He watched her watch him, her face a speculative, serious mask.

Then she spoke, cool and clear, ''Since it wasn't my fault, since you think I did a lot of good in what you consider a relatively short period, what was the past month really about?''

So here it was—the trap. She'd got him to pour it out, give credit and assign blame then—bam! How hadn't he seen it coming? Had he totally lost his IQ?

The real problem was, he had no answer. He had had the best of reasons to seek unity with GAO, and to insist on being in charge where La Clínica's running and the immediate contact with the community were concerned. Laura had been too zealous, demanding too rapid a change, not acquainted with people's natures, the daily volatile conditions and the totally different way of doing things in general here. He now knew who'd been responsible for her unrealistic attitudes.

But he hadn't had to treat her the way he had. He could have simply talked through his concerns, tutored her in some hard realities, split responsibilities, keeping her to the tasks she'd already proved adept at—cajoling the authorities, charming the media, drawing in donations through her high-society contacts—and been thankful for all that instead of resenting her for it. Most of all, he shouldn't have taken over her achievements.

He'd known he'd be much more valuable in GAO's eyes, that he'd be more effective far more quickly than her when given access to their leverage. And he'd used that to exclude her.

He *had* been unreasoning, territorial, prejudiced. Scared.

And it had had nothing to do with the chain of command, ego or the general good.

It had had everything to do with her. He'd been scared to let her close. Scared of what he'd do. Scared he'd lose control and betray himself and his cousin.

Should he tell her the truth?

How could he? She despised him enough already!

Maybe if he offered, again, to make amends?

He looked at her as she shifted in the creaking swivel chair opposite his desk, emerald eyes incandescent in the sunlight pouring from his eastern window as she waited for his reply. Remote, unruffled. Disappointment lurched inside him.

She'd let him kiss her, had melted into him. With shock alone? Would her surface be so placid if he affected her the same way she affected him? Maybe he should press the point…

No. One reluctance at a time. One yes at a time.

Not pressing the point didn't mean not persuading, though.

He swiveled her around, leaned both arms on either side of her, his head coming closer to hers. He took his time, savoring the agonizing approach, soaking up her every nuance—the shimmers in her hair, the mouth-watering scent, the black pupils forcing the irises into strained green bands.

Good. A reaction. Whatever it was. Better than none.

"Contrary to common belief, Laura, I'm not infallible."

Pull him down and finish that kiss.

Laura would have laughed if she hadn't been choking on her heart. That voice inside her head was going crazy. Maybe *it* was having that breakdown. Could pregnancy's haywire hormones be responsible for that too?

Yes. Probably. Hopefully.

She stared up at him. Oh, who was she kidding?

Him, reason urged. She had to kid him. It was too risky to let him read her. Good thing she had a lifetime of emotional exile for back-up. Her perfected, opaque façade would throw his mind-probing off track.

Tease him. Keep it light. She smiled, adjusting her mask. "There. It didn't hurt that much, now, did it? So, now we know you're human, now you've—insert gasps of shock here—admitted you were less than fair, wrong even, care to define your earlier promise of restructuring our working relationship in solid terms?"

He smiled back. Her mask teetered. He really should be banned from smiling in inhabited areas. "In writing, if you like," he said, leaning even closer, his voice, his scent invading her every intimate thought and place. "Let's write a contract. Let's write two…"

Armando's older assistant, Maria, burst in unannounced with coffee.

Oh, thank you! Laura gulped gratefully at the respite. But not for long. Soon fury replaced agitation. Maria was devouring Armando's suggestive pose above her, no doubt stocking ammunition for the ribald gossip sweeping La Clínica. The people here had no respect—no concept of privacy!

But, then, Armando wanted everyone to buy into a raunchy affair between them. Part of his plans to marry her and claim the baby for his own.

And there he was, playing the sultan again, directing Maria to pour his coffee while towing *her* to the beat-up leather sofa by the window. Marry him? Ha. She'd refused to go through with marrying Diego at the first sign of conflict. And a good thing she'd insisted, too. Otherwise she would have been even more disillusioned, not to mention a widow. Now…

Now she was *only* an unmarried mother-to-be!

Armando dismissed Maria and sat down beside Laura, pouring then handing her her coffee.

Anger crackled. "I will need this contract, Armando," she snarled. "I can't trust you to even ask how I like my coffee!"

His smile was all indulgence, his ebony eyes following her move as she gulped down a much-needed mouthful. "Almost all cream, three spoons of sugar, filled-to-spilling mug." At her gasp he added a sultry three-word caress. "I watch you."

The coffee missed its normal route down her throat. "You don't!" she spluttered. "At least, you didn't. You never looked at me."

"So how come I know how you take your coffee?"

How indeed? What was going on here? Did he really mean what his eyes were saying? Had that kiss been for more than getting his own way and proving how irresistible he was?

His resonant purr softened even more. "Will you stop considering me your enemy, Laura?"

She put the mug down. It could prove fatal, drinking coffee around that confounding man. Suddenly she remembered to what lengths he went to achieve his objectives. His new ones were her surrender and his name on her baby's birth certificate. This could all be a ruse.

"I won't—until proven otherwise, if you don't mind."

"*Querida*, I've asked you to marry me. I'm conceding your equal right to running operations and La Clínica as long as it's GAO-sponsored. What more proof can I give you?"

Distaste chilled through her at the echoes of Diego's crooning Spanish endearments. "How about starting by not *querida*-ing me and treating me like an equal? Like you would a male colleague."

"We have a saying here, *querida*." He stressed the endearment again, injecting it with a huskiness that shuddered through her. "Loosely translated, 'If you want to be obeyed, don't order the impossible'."

"I can see that *this* is going to be impossible." She jumped up to her feet, cursing her trembling limbs. "I had the right idea two weeks ago, that day of the riot. I only picked the wrong day to arrange for my departure."

He came after her, already snaring her back into his orbit. *Go away,* she wanted to scream. *I need to think and you're denying me access to my own mind!*

Both their beepers went off.

So God was still listening to her prayers!

Turning to her escape route, she found him blocking it.

"Move out of my way, Salazar."

"Why? I thought you wanted to leave."

"I'll see what the emergency is first."

"No, you won't. You're either a part of this or you're not. If you plan to walk out some time, walk out now."

Walk out—and go where? And to whom? A job in some surgical department or private-sector center back home? That was no option. Retracing her father's curtailed footsteps in aid work had been why she'd become a doctor. As for family and friends—what family and friends? She could still ask GAO to relocate her, but—

"Until you decide if you're in or out, I have a job to do."

She caught him as he turned away, fingers digging into his arm. "I'm in. And you'd better understand that when I sign up for a job, I'm in all the way!"

"I know it's far out of your usual reach, Dr. Salazar, but—"

"We go to an emergency wherever it is, Fernando," Armando cut off the man's stumbling words, reaching for the bag full of emergency drugs and supplies Lucianna handed him. "It's just a longer flight."

Just a longer flight? Even Laura, with her sketchy knowledge of Argentinian geography, knew Monte FitzRoy was at the southern end of Argentina. It would take La Clínica's only fixed-wing plane at least six hours to get there.

"Let's hope a closer emergency service reaches them first," Armando continued as he strode out to the short runway at the back of La Clínica, Laura and the team gathered for the emergency running behind him.

"Everyone said it was doubtful they could send anything!"

Fernando gasped, barely keeping up with them. "It's tourist season and they're busy elsewhere…"

"Whatever the situation, we'll do all we can and get Juan and Rosalia back home to you."

"Thank you, thank you so much, Dr. Salazar—"

Armando interrupted him again. "*Por Dios*, Fernando, it's Armando and don't thank us yet—or at all. It's our job."

Twenty minutes later, they were sitting in a row on the plane, Constanza, Armando, her, Jason then Susan. On the other side were two stretchers. *La Bianca* was the best plane La Clínica used. Laura was impressed to find it as well equipped as the best she'd ever seen, with low-profile sleds for maximum patient access, intubation seat, loading lights, oxygen, compressed air, suction, AC/DC power, storage bays, heated IV bins and locking drug boxes.

A local businessman had turned it into aeromedical transport at La Clínica's disposal when their emergency team had saved his son after a nearly fatal boating accident. In fact, all the aircrafts La Clínica used were either donations or bought at clearance auctions. GAO was supposed to put another highly equipped air ambulance craft, a rotor-wing this time, on La Clínica's fleet, and Laura was determined to make that soon.

"This isn't the usual mountain-climbing accident, people." Armando interrupted her thoughts, his explanations directed to the ones who hadn't attended Fernando Aguilera's frenzied report. "Fernando had a hysterical call from his daughter-in-law an hour ago. She and her husband were part of a mountain-climbing team of eight who were mapping out possible routes for their tourist programs. Two of their number went missing. After a frantic search for them, they found them, both injured gravely, injuries they'd inflicted on each other."

Constanza whistled. "How ridiculous to go to the top of the world along with someone you want to kill!"

"Not just along, but someone you must trust with your life

in case anything goes wrong.'' Susan, who was a climber herself, shook her head in disbelief.

''It seems there's a romantic triangle involved and the males decided to fight it out.'' Armando said. ''Then the woman whose man was fighting over another woman—that's Fernando's daughter-in-law—decided to get even with her rival. When the dust settled, they had three injured who needed emergency intervention. Just like in many tragedies, fate went for overkill. Cellphones didn't work and they gained another injury on the way down—a broken leg. They still managed to descend and hike to El Chalten, the small town at the foot of Monte FitzRoy. Unfortunately, the town's clinic wasn't equipped to handle such injuries. They put the call out to many emergency services from there, including us.''

''If they survive this, they should turn it into a screenplay and sell it to Hollywood!''

Laura's words were her last for the next three hours.

During those hours, Constanza had Armando's ear firmly glued to her mouth. Laura couldn't help but hear the conversation—the monologue more like—though she missed most of it as Constanza had slipped back into Spanish. But there was one thing she got for sure. Constanza wanted Armando. Badly.

Another certainty hit her at the same time. She hadn't had him.

Fierce satisfaction hit her as hard. Harder. Why should she care who'd had and who hadn't had Armando? Anyway, it was probably just because Armando didn't get involved with colleagues.

But *she* was his colleague, so why…?

A wrench crunched in her unaccustomed feminine ego trip. Diego's baby! That was why.

For the rest of the trip, they slept, had a meal, went over their inventory of supplies and prepared for any contingency. With no coherent report transmitted, they had no idea what injuries to expect.

On the last leg of the flight Laura's growing impatience was forgotten as she looked out of the window and gaped at the sheer, humbling majesty of the dramatic peaks below them.

"That's Cerro Torre mountain there." Armando's voice suddenly purred in her ear. "Its neighbor, Monte FitzRoy, is where we'll land. They're both part of the Fueguinos Andes that extend like a huge wall, a natural border with Chile."

"How can you tell which mountains we're above?" She turned to gape at him in turn.

"You mean you didn't see the colossal names painted all over them?" he teased. "Still finding it hard to read Spanish, *querida*?"

"There are parachutes on this plane, right?"

"Don't push me out yet. Who'll name mountains for you if you do?"

"Don't worry, I'll enjoy the scenery without putting labels on it."

"You may be right. Patagonia is how Earth used to be millions of years ago, rolling from the awe-inspiring Andes to the plateau steppe lands to the Atlantic at its most daunting in the east. And in between the lakes, the glaciers, the rivers and valleys and pines and magnificent wildlife. It's a humbling experience, looking at its sheer majesty."

Laura started. Her own thoughts. He *was* a mind-reader!

She shook away the spooky moment. "You make a good guide. You may live."

She savored the light moment and his chuckle. She had a feeling there wouldn't be any more for a long time to come.

As soon as they landed on a tiny landing strip outside El Chalten, they rushed to its only clinic, where their casualties were.

The moment they entered, a woman screamed, "Why are you here?" The tall, stout woman launched herself at them, for some reason targeting Laura in demented fury. "You incompetent, useless fools! You're too late! *Too late*, you hear?"

Armando extricated Laura from the disheveled woman's talons, growling a frightening rebuke in Spanish that had her bursting into hysterical wailing. But at least it got her out of their way so they'd waste no more time getting to their patients.

One was already going into rigor mortis.

The bloody bandages on his temple detailed his most probable cause of death.

"Juan—Fernando's son." Armando abruptly gave the stiffening man's identity.

The woman's husband—her cheating husband. And he'd died fighting over his mistress. How sad. Laura could forgive her the deep bruises she felt forming on her arms. To love and lose like that, in every way. Like her father. But at least he hadn't known…

"Laura!" Armando's call dragged her to the present. "You and Susan handle the woman there. Constanza and Jason, handle the broken leg. I'll see to the man."

Laura wanted to protest getting the less urgent casualty, but didn't. Armando was the more experienced emergency doctor.

As soon as she saw her charge, she knew why the woman had attacked her. Long black hair, same build, light eyes—*eye*, one being covered with a blood-soaked compress—but blue instead of green. The resemblance was strong enough to act as a red flag to someone crazed with grief and betrayal.

But whatever resemblance there had been in features, it was impossible to tell now. The woman's face was shredded to a swollen pulp, far worse than Laura's had been after her accident.

"Señora?"

The woman made no indication she'd heard, a huddled mass in the corner at the foot of an examination bed.

Shock. Or sedation.

"Susan—10 mg each diazepam and morphine." Just in case it was the first. She couldn't risk her coming out of it and going berserk in the middle of stitching.

Laura turned to one of the woman's friends. "What's her name, *señor*?"

"Isabella. Rosalia just tore and tore at her…" The man looked about to heave.

"Did Rosalia hit her on the head? Did Isabella fall?" Laura asked, trying to exclude head injury as the cause of the woman's stupor.

"It happened in a second—Rosalia just jumped on her and the blood was all over her hands and…" The man whimpered again. "We—we dragged Rosalia away and—and Isabella was still standing, her face covered in blood, screaming she was blind…"

That was all Laura needed to know. "Go and rest, *señor*. We'll take care of her."

One of the clinic's two medics approached. Good. Now, if only he spoke enough English to tell them if and how much sedation he'd administered. Armando and Constanza were too preoccupied to help. The man did speak English, just enough.

"Stop blood. No drug. You give?" the old man said.

Yes, indeed. "Go ahead with the injections, Susan."

Afterwards, they laid Isabella down and gave her a quick overall check to ascertain there were no other major injuries.

"The pressure bandage to her bleeding eye wounds wasn't a good idea," Susan muttered as she worked off the tape sticking the offending dressing in place. "Extra pressure could prove disastrous if the eye itself is injured."

Laura could only agree. More so as they got their first look at Isabella's eye.

So *that* was why her friend had been about to pass out. Laura heaved in a steadying breath, hearing Susan's indrawn "Oh, Gawd!"

"Could just be severe lid trauma. Let's hope for the best," Laura said, evading Susan's I-don't-think-so look.

In seconds Susan had the irrigating, disinfecting and suturing materials at her gloved fingertips as they flitted in quick, light dabs, clearing the congealed blood obscuring the woman's whole eye orbit, investigating the true extent of the damage.

"No need for visual acuity or eye movement tests, I guess," Susan breathed. "This is as bad as it could be."

And it was. Full-thickness jagged tears in both upper and lower lids, total conjunctival hemorrhage, cornea visibly torn and already hazing up, pupil distorted and unreactive to light, eye globe itself sunken with diminished pressure.

"Oh, Lord, is that a nail hooked in the sclera?" Susan gasped.

Laura's stomach protested again as she nodded. The sclera, the white part of the eye, was really tough. For nails to penetrate it…Rosalia must have been out to kill.

"Her husband lost a few teeth, his jaw's broken as well as seven ribs." Laura raised her head from contemplating the best methods of intervention at Armando's quiet words. "I sedated and intubated him, but the hemothorax had already clotted so I couldn't drain it. He'll last until we can open him up and evacuate the clot. Apart from killing a man and ruining his life for ever, he'll be all right. The broken leg is a straight-forward simple tibia-fibula fracture. He'll be all right, too."

Laura transferred her eyes from his to Isabella. "She'll never be all right again."

He shook his head in regret, his eyes again those empathetic weapons of devastation. "Can you handle it?"

She swallowed, nodded. "I took an ophthalmic surgery round during my internship."

Armando leaned over and inspected Isabella's eye. "Scleral and corneal interruption and foreign body impaction," he murmured. "There isn't much to do beyond preventing infection and further loss of intraocular pressure. I don't think you should remove the nail and risk more vitreous loss. She's also a prime candidate for endophthalmitis. Not to mention tetanus from those scratches."

Endophthalmitis was the most catastrophic event that could occur, turning the vitreous humor—the viscous fluid filling the eye and giving it its shape and pressure—into pus and destroying the eye beyond repair.

"Prophylactic broad-spectrum antibiotics and a tetanus booster, Susan," Laura directed, then looked at Armando. "I thought like you at first, but if we wait until we get her back to La Clínica to intervene surgically, we'd be performing enucleation and removing her eye instead of repairing it!"

He went still. "You think so?"

"Yes."

His eyes locked on hers for a moment, then he looked around, a torrent of Spanish spilling from his lips, sending all present flying, doing his bidding.

In under fifteen minutes, they were back at the plane with their patient, getting ready for the emergency operation and scrubbing up as best they could with the available facilities.

Nervousness and much more churned inside Laura. She'd repaired a ruptured globe only once. But it was what Armando had done that was really throwing her off balance. He'd taken her word, no arguments! Would she ever figure him out?

After they draped Isabella, leaving only the operative field exposed, he looked at her. "I've never done eye surgery, so it's up to you."

And it was, wasn't it? Everything seemed up to her.

"Where do you want me?" he asked.

An answer almost escaped. Unprofessional, provocative—not to mention crazy. Laura bit her tongue and pretended to consider who'd be her assistant, looking from Jason and back to him, as he'd done with her and Constanza.

When she answered him, she was appalled to hear herself saying, "You're already exactly where I want you."

CHAPTER SIX

"Is THIS all you'll do, now you got me where you want me?"

Laura read the sculpted lips inches from hers. Her head filled with a drowning drone, her body with heated urges from the formidable body rocking against her. She succumbed to one of them.

She traced pure, rugged power beneath stubbled bronze skin, her finger snagging in a faint cleft. Then in a set of white incisors.

Sharp pleasure slammed into her—then a growl. She heard the words this time.

"Wake up, Laura."

She started, blinking, disoriented. It took one more second, then she re-entered reality with a thud.

She was still on *La Bianca*. And she was all over Armando—again.

This time his arms were all over her, too.

"Do continue your exploration, now that you're awake."

No answer formed in her fogged mind. *Sit up, pull away.* She did, and almost fell back in his arms when for a second he tightened his hold. Then he let her go. His soft chuckle trickled down her simmering nerve endings. "It's true, then— all you want to do is sleep on me."

She stretched her aching back and stitch-laden sides. "And you make one hard and uncomfortable mattress."

He chuckled louder this time, worsening the effect. "She slumps over me, paralyzes me until I'm stiff and sore, and *she's* complaining. Tough customer."

She made a face at him and sat forward to get a better look at Isabella. She was in the same position she'd been in since the end of her operation, intubated, on breathing support and fully sedated.

"She's fine, and so's her husband, as far as anyone can be fine in these circumstances." Armando softly squeezed her shoulder, handed her a mug of coffee.

"Oh, thanks." Suddenly, those moments when she'd made that audacious comment and his answering flare of sensual challenge came back to her with full force. What had happened to the Armando she'd abhorred four weeks ago? Or the woman who'd thought she'd never know anything but her same old gray existence?

He's not who you thought he was. And he makes you someone you didn't know you could be. What happens when you revert to normal again? Or is this who you really are?

He was saying something.

"What?"

"If you're not awake yet, just say so!"

"Will you just be a gentleman and repeat the question? Or is that beyond you?" she snapped.

"Being an ogre, I'd say it is. But again—just because I want the answer—do you think Isabella has a chance of retaining any eyesight?"

"I think so. I couldn't get a good look at the fundus though the hazy cornea, but I think we caught the vitreous loss early enough for it not to cause significant retinal damage. Usually when too much is lost and the intraocular pressure is severely lowered, the retina gets detached, or expulsive hemorrhage— literally spewing the eye contents outwards—results. Though Rosalia has done a lot of damage, it wasn't as bad as, say, what a collision trauma would have caused. It was confined to the anterior segment of the eye, where repair is easier and yields better results. Visual acuity will depend on a successful keratoplasty first, though, to implant a new cornea instead of the one that was shredded."

His smile widened at her detailed report. "I hereby appoint you the eye doctor of the Argentina Project!" A soft pinch of her cheek accompanied his amused words. She felt his touch right down to her bones.

"I appoint myself, if you don't mind!"

"Who's developing a case of last worditis now?"

The plane suddenly dipped and lurched. Armando's smile disappeared as he took the mug from her, disposed of the remaining coffee, pushed her back into her seat and tightened her seat belt. He must have loosened it when she'd slid sideways over him.

"Isabella." Her eyes flew to their patients.

"They're securely harnessed, and the stretchers and everything else are welded to the floor," he reassured her. "Sit back. Susan, put that plate and fork in the locking cabinet beside you. You can finish your cake when this passes."

But the air turbulence didn't pass. It got violent. Then frightening. Then beyond even that.

Long moments later, Laura was almost gagging on the stench of doom permeating the air. Surely the plane couldn't stand being battered this way for much longer? It heaved and plummeted and almost rattled apart. Then suddenly it made one full, vicious flip.

Terror lodged in her throat, went unscreamed. Susan's came out on a shrill shriek. "We're gonna fall!"

"Get a grip, Suz!" Jason, sounding as scared as Susan, broke off on an involuntary shout as the plane nosedived, then spiralled downwards, out of control.

This was it. They *were* falling. Laura's breath burnt in her chest, nausea and fear and helplessness paralyzing her, her frantic eyes slamming around to the others as they were flung against her and against each other, desperate for anything— some sort of reassurance. Their conditions only deepened her dread. Susan was vomiting, Jason trying—and failing—to help her, barely hanging on himself, Constanza was spastic in her chair, eyes closed, lips trembling, praying, it seemed. And Armando…

He betrayed none of the outright terror of the others, but he was tense, intense. Face taut, jaw clenched, eyes fierce—and on *her*. He rammed into her in the next violent pitch. She welcomed the collision, completed it, surged into him.

He snatched at her, crushing her into a bruising hug. She whimpered with relief. She needed that, needed the haven that was him. It was crazy, ridiculous, but suddenly she felt she could face dying as long as he was there with her.

"Don't be afraid, *querida*," he breathed into her ear as she squashed her face in his neck, hanging onto his solid body. "Romero is one hell of a pilot, and we've had worse flights than this."

"And I thought you were a good liar, Armando," she choked.

"You did, eh, *poca una*? Is there any vice I don't possess in your eyes?"

"Besides being a ruthless, remorseless, patronizing, prejudiced, despotic, holier-than-thou…"

"So you're not scared after all! You can't be and come up with all those adjectives!"

"Who's coming up with anything? I'm reciting from memory." She dug her fingers into him, hugging him frenziedly through another flip. "We're going to die, aren't we, Armando?"

He didn't answer, just tipped her head back and took her panting lips.

For ever—she'd waited for ever to feel him this way again, sharing his breath, tasting his life, opening to his dominance—for ever and less than a day.

She no longer felt anything but him. If she were to die, what better way to die than in Armando's arms? Nothing else mattered…

Nothing but one thing! Her baby. Her baby had to grow, to be born, to live. She *couldn't* die! And she had to give it the best future. The best father.

Armando.

"Do you still want to marry me?" she gasped into his

mouth. He just kissed her harder, devouring her question, her lips, again and again.

"Is that a yes?" He deepened their merging for answer, growling into her throat.

"You haven't asked me in a week!"

"Laura *Loca*!" He actually laughed, withdrew to bury his lips in her neck as the plane plunged again. "Laura *Loca* with your *preguntas locas*!"

"They're not crazy questions!" She squeezed her eyes shut, terror almost suffocating her. "Just answer me."

"Yes, Laura, I still want to marry you. I haven't proposed again since last week, because I thought a biweekly basis looked better. Satisfied?"

"Then I accept. I want to marry you as soon as we land. If we land."

They landed.

How, she didn't know. Armando had been right, as usual. Romero was one hell of a pilot. He didn't seem to think there'd been much danger.

Weather conditions on the ground were even worse.

"Is this a hurricane?" Jason shouted above the roaring wind, almost choking on the torrent pelting them, drenching them to the bone in a second.

They were struggling against the brutal wind as they ran from the runway to the seemingly deserted La Clínica's back entrance. Armando's massive body ahead of Laura's took the brunt of the elements, his grasp as he led the way reassuring. Not so his answer. "There've been no alerts. Still, you can't second-guess nature, especially nowadays, with global warming. And with this rain…" He let his words hang as they reached the door, giving them an even more disturbing import.

Far from being deserted, inside La Clínica, the work pace had escalated from brisk to hectic.

Lucianna and many others came rushing up to them, all directing rapid-fire reports and demands at Armando. He listened for a minute then turned back to his group, clapped his hands once, loud, decisive. "Right. Go dry off, everyone. Get some rest, too. Everything will carry on without you for a couple more hours." Then he rushed after Lucianna.

Laura clung to his arm. "What about you?"

"I'll see to the most urgent things first."

"Oh, another superhero syndrome flare-up, right?"

"You're just jealous they want me and not you!" Armando added speed to his steps, forcing her to run after him, his words muffled as he whipped his soggy sweatshirt over his head.

Laura's retort fell apart, right along with her every cerebral function.

Next moment she was again plastered against that living bronze expanse, a rough kiss forcing her open mouth even wider. "I'll take care of everything. Then I'll invite everyone. You go get ready for our wedding, *querida*."

Warm water ran down her body, soothing her flesh instead of fusing suffocating clothes to it. Tropical fruit scents permeated her senses instead of dank, stifling nerves and overwork. Her shower cubicle's watertight isolation cocooned her in peace.

None of it was working.

She'd been less scared on that plane, counting down her remaining moments of life!

Thinking she was plummeting to her death had a lot to answer for. And Armando, opportunity-hunter that he was, was keeping her to the letter of her promise! She'd said she'd marry him as soon as they landed, hadn't she?

Go get ready for our wedding, he'd said.

How did she prepare for something that would change everything, for ever?

She didn't even have a dress!

Panic kicked her eyes open, only for shampoo to force them closed with scalding tears.

"Stupid, ridiculous, moronic!" she spluttered, rinsing her eyes vigorously then stamping out of the cubicle.

A *dress*? She, Laura Burnside, panicking about her lack of dresses? Next she'd be going to pieces over her bouquet color!

"You, *idiot*, are a thirty-two-year-old pregnant woman," she spat at her reflection. "You look like hell, you've shed half your flesh and you've turned into a harpy to boot. You're not a bride, this isn't a real marriage…"

The little demented voice infiltrating her logic circuits interrupted.

Who says this isn't a real marriage?

"This isn't a real marriage, is it?"

It was just four hours later, and Armando was standing in the middle of her rented villa's gigantic reception room, shaking off the rain from his wealth of mahogany hair and acre-wide shoulders, his grandeur making her feel tiny and drab. As if that wasn't enough, the amused indulgence in his onyx eyes made her feel even smaller.

Did he have to look so…so…? And a formal suit too? At least it wasn't a tuxedo. She had to be thankful for non-existent blessings. Oh, for heaven's sake!

Fighting the urge to go and hide somewhere, beneath her bed preferably, she told herself those pastel green jeans and jumper were the best she had, and they would have to do. She hadn't been planning on hitting the social circles in Argentina after all.

It didn't work. She still wished she'd vanish.

Armando's tactile gaze slithered over her heaving breasts, lingered, then rose again, probing her down to her cellular level.

"You're really asking do I want sex?" He laughed. Oh, Lord! He really, really shouldn't be allowed to do that around poor females. "What do *you* think?" He waited a beat then his voice dipped to a deep, drowning caress. "Yes, Laura, I want sex. Plenty of long, hot, *hard* sex."

She almost coughed her lungs out. He prowled towards her, gathered her to his chest, delivering firm thumps between her shoulder-blades. "Relax, *querida*. My offer of marriage stands even if you don't want it. It's up to you, OK?"

"But—but when I said…" No words formed in her mind. A rare occurrence.

"When you said you'd marry me, you thought we'd plunge to our deaths and you wouldn't have to go through with it. And then you thought I'd want a marriage of convenience, just my signature on a piece of paper right under yours. Am I getting hotter?"

"Sizzling!" she sputtered.

"So again, Laura, I'm easy. Very. You want me, come and get me. You don't, I won't come near you."

"Armando, I am totally confused here. Why?"

"Why not?"

"And if I don't want…? What would you be doing for—for…"

"Relief? I'm a grown man, don't worry about me."

"You mean you'll…!"

"*Do* try to complete a sentence, *querida*. You sound like a censored sound track. And, no, I don't mean I'll…! As long as we remain married."

"You mean…" Damn. She *would* complete this question. "The marriage doesn't have to be permanent?"

He burst out laughing. She almost swooned. "You do wonders for a man's ego. No, Laura, it doesn't. I never intended to get married, but now I am for all the reasons you know, I *would* like it to work. If it doesn't, then it doesn't. No marriage should continue in any form if it isn't working."

"What does working mean exactly?"

"What do you want it to mean?"

"OK, let me rephrase the question. In *this* marriage, what would constitute 'working'?"

"Why don't we find out? Can you imagine a better bargain?

What other man would give you all the benefits of marriage and leave it up to you where its commitments are concerned?''

"Maybe you sound too good to be true!"

He was pure devilry now. "I am."

Right now, she believed it. And how!

He sobered just a bit. "Listen, Laura, it *is* up to you! You already know that or you wouldn't have made that crack about having me where you wanted me. So why not quit having those distrust relapses?''

"If only you'd give me a reason I could buy! No matter how pragmatic your motives, how open your expectations, you *are* making a huge commitment to someone you don't even like…''

"Didn't, past tense. Now I do. And what's more important, I *want* you.''

"You must want a thousand other healthy, reasonably attractive females!''

His laughter boomed again. "Even *I* am not that prolific. But anyway, those females are not carrying my cousin's child, neither are they integral to my work.''

So that was it, wasn't it? Sex, baby, work! More than enough reasons for marriage. In his view. Marriage was clearly more elastic in his book than in hers. Love, devotion, permanence didn't enter into his equation.

But why should they? They no longer seemed like plausible prerequisites to her. His reasons made sense, tangible, irrefutable sense. Hers were platitudes that had emptied her life and shriveled her heart. It said much about her judgement that she'd reached her age with only her failed relationship with Diego to account for the sum total of her emotional involvements. Maybe *she'd* alienated everyone all her life, thwarted herself, asked for too much.

She looked at him. Really looked, beyond the blinding virility. Powerful, in control, unpretentious. A helpmeet with the same goals, a man without hidden agendas, desire without false expectations and freedom if and how she wanted it. His offer *was* too good to be true.

Was *he*?

She couldn't wait to find out.

The smile on Armando's face was getting heavier, his muscles creaking in agony under its weight. Just a few more seconds and it would crack and crash. Maybe he should let it. If this was what he was letting himself in for, this struggle, this…torture, maybe he should run and never look back. Meet her at work like any other colleague, involve himself in her baby's life as a doting uncle, go drown in a woman or twenty and deplete his lust for her. If every unintentional touch did this to him, if every inch of trust, every atom of approval took that much out of him, he shouldn't be doing this. Was this how it felt to be digging your own grave?

And for what? Sticking around and finding out for sure how she didn't want him in return? Giving her every chance to keep on rejecting him on a daily basis?

It isn't too late, self-preservation urged. *Tell her she's right, that it won't work, and work something else out.*

"So, where do you get married around here?"

The tension bracing him for her reaction vanished, the drain sickening. This was more reason to end it here and now!

But she's agreed, asking to get married. Snatch her and run to the altar before she changes her mind.

This was getting scary. He used to have control, reason—distance.

Cool it, Salazar. You've been cool all your life. Fake it now.

He let go of the smile before he hurt himself. His voice didn't sound like his own any more, but at least he managed an even "In a church, *querida*. Where else?"

"You may now kiss the bride."

Armando spoke the words, slow and clear, his rich, powerful tones distinct even over nature's tumult.

He was translating to her—and to the priest.

But the priest hadn't been relying on his accuracy. He'd kept asking her in the most mutilated English if she was saying what she thought she was saying. The small congregation's snickers had risen, especially her teammates', relishing Armando's discomfiture. Not that he *was* discomfited.

He was dazzling, a figure out of her most lavish fantasies as he towered over her, holding both her hands in his all through the ceremony, reciting the wedding vows in Spanish then in English. And he'd just pronounced them man and wife and was about to seal it all with a kiss.

Thunder had been crashing at the small chapel's walls, wind and rain banging millions of hysterical fists against its boarded windows. Then Armando lowered his head and suddenly everything hushed.

Then he raised his head. And having gathered its breath, nature exploded into an even more frightening, sustained crescendo.

But what frightened her was what kept happening to her whenever he kissed her. She felt possessed, drained, lost. He stared at her and the sensation deepened. Then he suddenly smiled, relinquishing his eerie hold over her senses. "Quite a soundtrack, eh?" He pressed her hand to his lips, a lingering kiss fusing his ring to her finger. "So—ready to go, Señora Salazar?"

She searched for her voice, found a tremulous croak instead. "Demoted from Doctor to Señora already?"

He raised one formidable eyebrow, then just hugged her to his side, steering her from the altar and back among the two rows of wedding guests.

With congratulations over, he made a mad dash to his four-by-four with her swept high and protesting in his arms so she wouldn't muddy herself. Once he'd got her out of the rain, he wasn't in a hurry to escape it himself. At his door, he took his time, taking off his soaking jacket and throwing it in the back. By the time he discarded his tie, her mouth was as dry as his white dress shirt was wet, and not leaving much to memory.

So that was the attraction of wet shirt contests! Provided they were populated by men like him. If there *were* any more men like him.

And he was her husband now. *Her husband.*

She had every right to obey that painful itching in her hands, to reach out and assuage it by contact with his flesh…

"Don't you think two Dr. Salazars would be confusing?"

She blinked. What…? Oh! So he hadn't been ignoring her earlier comment.

She used the moments while he revved the motor and waved to the colleagues who were already departing in the other direction to dampen her heated fantasies. Then she turned to him. "There'll only be one Dr. Salazar—me!" She heard the provocation in her voice, was helpless to control it. "Aren't you just Armando, Mr. First-name-basis-with-everyone? If you don't approve, I'll just keep my maiden name, thank you."

That perpetual glint in his eyes flared. What was she doing, playing with this kind of fire? What if he considered her teasing an invitation? Was it? What would she do if he took her up on it?

She had to make up her mind fast. He was leaning over her, his fresh breath scorching across her burning face, his lips an inch from hers, his steel arm and chest less than that from suddenly stinging breasts and clenching abdomen.

He just buckled her seat belt and withdrew.

"Laura Salazar." He articulated the name on a smug purr. "You're not keeping your name. And people here will call you whatever they want, not what you tell them to call you. Want to guess what that will be?"

Señora Salazar.

The man on the phone had called her that.

Armando's eyebrows rose, questioning her descending ones as she handed him the handset.

After listening for a few seconds, his deepening dimples and his wink were an eloquent I-told-you-so. The Moroccan cushions on his sofa seemed like very good missiles. Right at the back of that majestic head he'd turned on her.

She was picking one up and pondering the wisdom of giving in to the urge when he ended the conversation and came up behind her.

Touch me! that wild persona taking over her mind and body almost cried out. *Just take me up those stairs to your bed. Don't give me the choice. I stink at choices. Take it out of my hands.*

He didn't even touch her. She turned to him, the cushion held close, a shield keeping her heart inside her ribcage.

A pointed look at the cushion, then back to her eyes. "That was your landlord."

"I gathered as much." A firmer squeeze on the cushion to hang onto something. "What did he want? And why didn't he tell *me* what he wanted? I'm his tenant, not you. Or does being Señora Salazar mean you're also my keeper?"

He waited out a boom of thunder, then shrugged. "You mentioned you wished you hadn't agreed to a six-month lease once." When? Not to him! To Diego, and she'd done it only once. He'd sulked so heavily then, she hadn't brought it up again. So how did Armando know? What else had Diego told him?

Armando was going on. "So I called Señor Delgado. We agreed that three days is enough time for you to vacate the place, then he'll come here for his key and to pay you back the three months' rent you've paid in advance."

Armando watched surprise chase away irritation on her vivid face. Then elation chased away everything else.

Was this how she looked when she was happy?

The sight entranced him. Hurt him. She'd looked only wary and reluctant when she'd repeated vows after him, her hand stiff and sweaty as he'd slipped his mother's wedding ring on her finger. She'd dropped his wedding band when she'd fumbled it on his finger.

Would she ever look this way for him?

The little whoop she gave oppressed him even more.

"Really? Oh, great! Oh, Armando, thanks! Señor Delgado was adamant about not repaying anything—in fact, he was downright nasty. How on earth did you manage it?"

What was she so happy about? Getting the three months' rent back? Money that was spare change to her? "I just asked him." He tried to curb his curtness, failed. "He agreed."

Her face dimmed, closed. "Must be an Argentinian thing, then. Or a man-to-man thing. Thanks anyway. And I'll call him back and tell him he can have the place and the keys back at once. Nothing of mine remains at the villa. Those two suitcases with me here are everything I have in Argentina."

"They are?" That surprised him—stunned him, even.

His mind tripped over her contradictions. She'd rented a villa big enough for a family of twenty then had bought a decrepit car for less than a two-month rental of a decent one. She'd come to Argentina with an exorbitant watch as a we-meet-at-last gift for Diego and a meager, utilitarian wardrobe. She'd come to their wedding in something a woman went shopping in. She came from a family with extensive money yet was ecstatic about getting back a few thousand dollars.

How did all that add up?

A comment Diego had once made suddenly came back to him. About her being tight.

He'd been shutting out anything Diego had been telling him about her. But that had registered. Probably because he'd been outraged Diego had dared make that comment. He'd told him only a gigolo or a pimp considered and complained about his woman's spending habits, when it was her money.

"So—is this place going to hold up?"

His focus snapped to the moment. The storm was as bad as

ever. "It's held up through four generations and a dozen hurricanes."

"Oh, that's great, then."

Suddenly he couldn't bear the unnatural squeak to her voice—and that damn cushion!

"You can put that cushion down, Laura. I'm not about to rip your clothes off and force myself on you."

"I know that," she protested, her voice regaining some of its usual authority and life.

Did she, now? Good thing one of them did. *He* sure as hell knew no such thing.

After today, after that kiss at the altar, after she'd put her ring on his finger and he'd promised to be hers for ever, he knew one thing. Keeping to his promise might be more than he could do.

The need for her, the pressure to overcome her reluctance, seduce her, was an expanding ache. He was certain with enough coaxing and stimulation he could—would. The idea of fondling her until she lost all reason and begged for release, of watching her in the throes of satiation, again and again, was sweeping him. The lust was spreading beyond the physical, corroding his heart, his soul.

Yet the need for her to come to him, to look happy for him, was far more consuming. He—he— *Dios l'ayuda…*

He loved her.

"Armando, for heaven's sake." She threw the cushion down on the sofa and looked up at him, hesitant, heartbreaking, his at last—and not his at all. "Don't look at me like that!"

He had no idea how he remained on his feet. How he found his voice. "How am I looking at you, *querida*?"

"How did you once put it? As if I'd sprouted another head!"

She remembered his words. Funny, that. "You've just sprouted a ridiculous schoolgirl expression. Not your style at all." *Enough. Take your eyes off her, get away from her. Now!*

He did. Turned on his heel, headed for the stairs. "I'm taking a shower then heading to La Clínica—night shift. *Bienvenida a su hogar nuevo,* Laura. Welcome to your new home."

He ran up the spiral stairs as if he were escaping eternal damnation. He at least escaped the gaze that followed him until he was out of her sight.

But there was no escaping her hold over him.

The bitterly funny part was that he'd condemned himself.

"And a happy wedding day to you too!" Laura said out loud the moment he disappeared. A laugh followed, incredulous and self-deprecating.

A night shift! That took care of any ridiculous schoolgirl jitters.

It was a good thing she hadn't obeyed that demented voice inside her, hadn't reached out and touched him. Her bridegroom, the man who'd said he wanted her just hours ago, had looked at her in horror, as if he'd just realized the real size of the catastrophe he'd brought on himself.

A night shift!

Had he scheduled it in his day today? Get back from emergency. Handle midday chores. Marry Laura. Deliver her to new parking space. Get on with rest of day.

Most probably. Since the prospect of more chaos in La Clínica seemed far more interesting than spending the night, their so-called wedding night, with her.

But what about tomorrow night? And from now on? Probably more of the same. Leaving it up to her to have a normal marriage no longer looked considerate or chivalrous. He probably did it because he could just as easily take her or leave her!

And she should be relieved, getting that marriage of convenience she'd thought the best solution. She wasn't. Not at all. She'd never even come close to being that disappointed in her life.

"Contrary, wacky…"

Her mumblings stopped. What was he doing, running down the stairs already? He must have skipped that shower.

He hadn't. He was glowing and as he passed her the whiff of cleanliness and man made her dizzy. He was at the door when she almost called out to him to say…anything. He talked first, his words delivered over his broad, receding shoulder. "The master bedroom is at your disposal, Laura. Later!"

Then he was gone into the storm.

Now, what was *that* supposed to mean? Master bedroom? Later?

One flight of stairs taken in threes later, her surge of agitated expectation fizzled to nothingness.

The master bedroom, where he'd put her luggage, was clearly not where he slept. It had been his parents' room, and she'd assumed he'd been using it since he'd come back to live here. He hadn't. But he'd got his husband-and-wife housekeeping team to prepare it for her, and on such short notice. It smelled good, the pastel sheets looked new, the curtains and the wall-to-wall carpet were clean. This was the room that had captured her imagination since she'd first seen it—king-sized bed, ten-foot-high ceiling, that bathroom with the tub under the skylight. Yet without imagining Armando there, it was as appealing as the splitting headache that was creeping down behind her eyes.

She wandered out and across the hall, following his scent. It led her to the furthest room on the second floor. Small, nearly empty. Just a single, very long bed, a two-door closet, a nightstand with a sad-looking lamp, the computer station in the corner the only thing that belonged to the last decade. This was where he slept. The place he'd made his own in his beautiful if rundown family home. Spartan, impersonal, bleak.

And a mess. Armando didn't have time to clean up after himself and only afforded his housekeepers once a week. Not too long ago he'd had his own elegant house, a brilliant career and financial prosperity. Now this was all he had left. The disheveled room blurred out of focus.

Accumulated tension and perpetual early pregnancy drowsiness overcame her. She sank onto his bed, the clamor of the elements accompanying her dry sobs and her disturbed surrender to slumber. She drifted, fiercely glad that his sheets hadn't been changed. She gathered them around her, sinking into his scent. It was the next best thing to sleeping with him...

Hands were dragging her away from her father.

No. He seldom came to her any more. It always hurt when he did, but she welcomed any pain that took her back into his arms, into security and love again. He'd been telling her things, and now she couldn't hear him. It was this horrible noise and these hands...

"No damn you! Let me go with him!"

"Laura!"

She opened her eyes to the sound of her own cry. And Armando's. He was there, above her—it was his hands she was struggling with. He'd come back!

"Armando..." She reached for the hands she'd been pushing away a second before. It was he who withdrew now. She followed, rising to her knees, shaking off her disorientation and grogginess. Then she saw it and it scared her. His face!

Twisted, gaunt, desolate. Or was it a trick of the light, the jagged yet almost continuous lightning slicing through the shutters?

No. It wasn't.

"Armando," she croaked again. "For God's sake, what is it?"

He lurched away when she sought reassuring contact with him. Her heart rammed the bottom of her throat. He seemed unable to talk. Was he injured?

She pounced on the bedside lamp, flicked it on and swung

to him, grasping his arms, her frantic eyes looking him over. He seemed OK, thank God. So what…?

He stumbled back, out of her reach, dragging both hands through dripping hair, plastering it more to his skull. ''I didn't find you in your room,'' he rasped. ''I thought you'd gone out there.''

That was why he looked so horrible? With fright? Over her? A chamber in her heart expanded, melted. ''Oh, Armando…''

''Then I realized you'd think the master bedroom was mine and you'd probably go and sleep in another room.'' Both hands rubbed his face, then he looked at her. He looked worse than when he'd been zapped by tear gas. ''You were weeping in your sleep. You sounded in so much pain, I thought—I thought you were miscarrying or something…'' He stopped, heaved in a huge breath, letting it out, shaking, labored.

He was so shaken up with concern for her? For her baby?

Just as Laura was about to throw herself at him and hug him for caring, for…just about everything, he told her the real reason behind his agitation.

''Anyway, you're fine so back to the reason I'm here. Rio Salado has flooded. Nearly twenty thousand people have been driven out of their homes in the last twelve hours. We got about fifteen thousand to official shelters. Until GAO moves in the morning, we have five hundred at La Clínica and three hundred more people with me downstairs who we need to set up for the night. Maybe indefinitely.''

CHAPTER SEVEN

"KEEP your money, Señor Delgado!"

Armando had just burst into his home, coming in from the torrential rain, soaked, with another two dozen stranded people in tow. He was in time to witness Laura's confrontation with the stodgy man in the middle of his jampacked reception area. Her voice was loud enough to carry over the agitated clamor of the crowd. He knew her reactions well enough to know she was struggling to suppress her distaste—and failing, barely keeping her tongue in check.

"I'm keeping the villa for the remainder of our contracted six months," she insisted.

"But I have new tenants," the man erupted. "Even people interested in buying it!"

"Well, you still have your money and I still have my contract. Until that expires, there's nothing more to say!"

She wants to run away, Armando thought, corrosive fingers clutching his heart. *Back to her luxurious villa.*

And he couldn't blame her. Going to work among chaos and desperation was one thing. But having those invade her so-called new home, on top of having to share it with him, her so-called new husband—it was no wonder she was giving up the money she'd been so happy to retrieve to have a refuge!

Señor Delgado kept his hand extended with the money, shaking it at her now, lapsing into angry Spanish. Two words hit Armando across the distance, even over the rising crowd's noise, raising his temperature to boiling point in a second. No one talked to Laura that way!

He cut through the distraught people milling in Reception, jumping over their heaped belongings, distributing apologies left and right for his rough haste. Then his angry momentum died in mid-stride. Laura had clutched the man's arm and was swinging him around, dragging him to one side and pouring a furious rebuke in his ear. The man turned livid as he listened, his uneasy glance darting around. At last he stuffed his money in his pocket, hesitated, got it out again, shoved it in her hands and bit off something short and adamant, then turned and hurried outside into the unrelenting rain to his car.

What had *that* been all about?

There was no time to wonder. Laura was heading towards him, deep in counting the money, exquisite dense eyebrows drawn together in concentration. She withdrew a few bills, put them in her pocket, then raised her head and smiled at him as she waded through the crowd, almost tripping over two running children.

He caught her and her smile grew. Another lance clear through him. He let her go as if she'd burned him. It had only been six hours since he'd admitted he loved her to himself. And he was still reeling. Even more from witnessing her turmoil in her sleep.

Let me go with him, she'd cried out.

Dios, had he been all wrong? Had she loved Diego? Even wished she'd died with him? Resented *him* for not letting her go with the man she'd loved?

What would he do now? What *could* he do?

"Here!" she said, tones still lilting. "That's Señor Delgado's contribution to the flood relief."

"But that's your money."

"No, it's his, since he's letting me keep the villa."

"Why would he do that?" He scanned her face in confusion. There was no sign of agitation there. Her eyes were no longer puffy and bleary with tears and loss, but the clear sable-lashed gems that went through his heart every time she looked at him. Like now. His hand went to his chest, pressing the familiar ache.

She gave a woman who was trying to placate her bawling baby a nod of deep sympathy and said, "Because I stepped hard on his every chivalrous and patriotic toe. I'm surprised but *very* grateful to say he has plenty of those.''

''You've lost me, *querida*!''

A resigned, long-suffering sigh. ''As big as this place is, three hundred plus people in it, with their stuff, even for a short while, is—as you can see—a mess. So, the villa is even bigger and will hold half of them until transit camps are set up or they're able to return to their homes. I know it's not much, but everything helps.''

''That's why you wanted to keep the villa?'' What was he asking? She'd already said so!

She gave him the ridicule he deserved. ''No, I'm going to leave you all squashed together here and go skip in twelve rooms on my own!''

What were you doing, skipping in them on your own in the first place? he almost blurted out. He didn't, *gracias Dios*. She had given it up, hadn't she? And her money... Well, she did keep some. Strange, that...

Stop! Just admit you're clueless where she's concerned and stop bashing your head against the wall!

''I called Howard Zimmerman, my GAO liaison in Santa Fe, and we've talked through sending in medical teams, relief supplies, water tanks, rescue boats and logistical kits to several sites. What did you do in your early morning shower?'' she asked, eyebrows still raised in lingering mockery.

''I organized things in La Clínica, got the distribution of food, mattresses and tents to official shelter camps going. I've also rounded up a team to investigate the situation and start search-and-rescue operations. I was only dropping off those people before heading out again.''

''*We're* heading out, you mean!''

''You're not even giving my request to take it easy consideration, are you?''

''No.''

Before he could growl a retort, or squash those sassy lips beneath his again, she turned to the packed reception area.

"Ladies and gentlemen—uh—your attention, please. We are moving half of you to another location, so those of you who are not comfortable here, if you will please gather your belongings and your families and come with us!"

The crowd hushed and gaped their incomprehension at her.

She turned help-me eyes to him, rousing the devil in him. "Did no one tell you that speaking slow, clear English doesn't make it understandable to people who don't know a word of it?" He received the expected discreet poke in the ribs with a taunting smile, then turned and translated to the crowd.

Soon they were leaving the people at Armando's home in the care of his housekeepers, Señor and Señora Amarilli, and going out into the downpour.

The cyclone had lessened in force, but the rain was heavier than ever. Most of those with them had had to wade out of their homes with almost nothing, only a lucky few having had time to drive away, or at least use boats to save some of their vital possessions. The bright side to that catastrophic loss was that the lack of belongings made it possible to cram a hundred and fifty people and their stuff into eighteen cars.

The roads were all awash in mud or water or both, and many times on the way to her villa they had to stop and haul stuck cars out of water ditches.

Laura watched in fascination as Armando organized the effort and in heart-pounding awe as his magnificent body flexed and bunched and heaved cars up. Then two cars broke down altogether. After failing to devise strong enough cables to tow them, they emptied them and slowed down to walking speed to accompany the people who got out and waded through the water.

Armando was livid when she insisted on taking her turn walking out there.

"Get in, Laura!"

"We still have ten miles to go. I'll walk a couple then alternate with you at the wheel."

"You won't be able to handle this car. Now, get *in*!"

"Why should I get preferential treatment over that pregnant woman over there, or those carrying babies and children?"

"*They* will rest at the end of this trek, you won't, as you insist! What good will you be to the thousands who need you now if you get ill? If you cause yourself even more permanent damage? Is this a superheroine flare-up? Just what are you trying to prove?"

"Maybe I'm after another headline!" She stumbled in the current and heard his explosive swearing. He stopped the car and the procession, flung open the door, hauled her inside and onto his lap.

"Not another word, Laura Salazar!" he growled, closing her protesting lips with a hard kiss, molding her to his side and driving on once more to the sounds of the pounding rain, the protesting engine and the passengers' chuckles.

Laura no longer heard anything but his heartbeats, felt nothing but him. She'd already melted somewhere between him hauling her up and her landing on his muddy lap. He swamped her, him and the memories. Memories of those moments when she'd thought he'd come back for her. She'd been disoriented, sure, but she'd been elated—ready for anything. Then he'd pulled away. She felt a *bit* better, knowing why he had.

Now he was clasping her, soiled, wet, disheveled and far more than anything she'd ever dreamed of. She had to be even closer, squeezed into his hardness, nestled her head into his neck.

He groaned her name. His tightening hold and hardening body left her pulseless, waiting for him to say something, promise anything—once all this was over. He said, promised nothing.

Nil visibility, she placated herself. *He has to concentrate on the road.*

After thirty more minutes of oppressive silence, they arrived at her villa. Howard Zimmerman was waiting there, sitting in his car with a local guide.

It took over an hour to get everyone and everything inside.

When everyone was relatively settled, they did their best at drying and cleaning up, then she directed Howard and Armando to the little kitchenette on the first floor, the only place they could have a quiet word in the overcrowded place.

"I understand congratulations are in order, Dr. Burnside," Howard said as he gratefully accepted a mug of tea.

At hearing her maiden name, she gave Armando a significant wink. And, oh, wow! Did that answering blaze in his eyes mean what she hoped it meant? What would she do if it didn't?

You'll work on him, that little delirious voice inside her urged. *Get him to make the first move, then...*

Fever. She must be coming down with something if all she could think of in her first ever natural disaster was seducing her husband.

That husband was brushing aside Howard's preliminaries and getting down to business in two sentences. "My last report was three hours ago. I expect the situation has worsened already?"

Howard's nod accompanied an eloquent sigh. "From last accounts numbers of displaced people have risen to forty thousand. Seven are reported dead, twenty-four missing. The number of displaced people hasn't been fully estimated yet, since a lot are taking shelter with relatives. A rough number's in the ballpark of fifty thousand. The local authorities are uncoordinated as yet, and far from having the situation under control. The 115 official shelters are just that at the moment, roofs over their heads. Not much is being offered there."

"I arranged for loads of food, clothes and mattresses to be distributed to those shelters," Armando said. "I assume the specific medicines and supplies I asked for are already on their way to La Clínica to be distributed?"

"Not everything you asked for was readily available..."

Armando bristled, and Laura intervened. "Our greatest priority now, Armando, is access to those who're still trapped on the roofs of their houses and in trees. There are thousands of them. And if the water rises again, the situation will worsen even further.''

Howard nodded again, clearly grateful to have Armando's focus distracted. ''Thirty-seven metric tons of emergency aid materials have already been dispatched, including the medicines on your list, hygiene and sanitation material, water-purification tablets, blankets, emergency shelters and cholera treatment kits. The additional relief materials and personnel Dr. Burnside requested—the volunteer teams of medical, logistical and water sanitation specialists—are *en route*.''

''What about the transit camp I asked GAO to set up outside La Clínica?'' Armando asked. ''The community drive we initiated has already accumulated enough provisions for ten thousand people. But if GAO doesn't set the camp up in the next few hours, those provisions will turn out to be a disaster instead. They're crowding La Clínica so that we can't take in more people!''

''We're doing all we can, Dr. Salazar,'' Howard said. ''But more roads are being cut off and this is slowing everything down. La Clínica, like this villa, is built on high ground and is not in danger, but not so the roads leading to them. The low-lying parts of the roads leading to La Clínica have been destroyed. It's very difficult to plan an intervention when everything should be done by helicopter or boat. And I'm sure you agree that all those available should be used for rescue at the moment!''

Armando closed his eyes for a full minute. When he opened them, it seemed he had everything worked out in his mind.

He rapped out his plan. ''OK, Zimmerman, transmit this to GAO. All operatives are to remain in *constant* contact with me. During the floods the province will be unrecognizable and your guides won't be of much help. I'm your best bet of finding your way around and reaching the most affected areas. Anyone who isn't directly involved in rescue operations is to arrange temporary health stations in these places…'' He flicked out a list from his back pocket. ''Liaise with the Health

Ministry and stress epidemic prevention. With the pollution of water sources, we're looking at possible cholera, malaria and measles outbreaks.''

Laura's cell phone rang. She answered, acutely aware of Armando's eyes on her, hanging on her every word, his crackling impatience to learn what was going on tangible—then audible. He kept intervening, telling her what to say, what to ask for. He was as pushy and controlling as he'd ever been, but now she saw it all through his eyes. The eyes of a man born to lead, to protect. It was even what his name meant: Armando, the Protector!

She gave reports and made demands, hers as well as his, her eyes helpless on his every twitching facial muscle. He was taking all this so very hard. It figured. Seeing his beloved, proud country and people being knocked down when they were already on their knees must be gutting him. Nothing he could do, nothing he *was* doing must seem enough. She concluded the conversation and turned to him.

''GAO Central has already sent La Clínica's new helicopter and another two pulled from an emergency service, with qualified rescue pilots bringing them over from Buenos Aires as we speak. There are also twenty rescue trucks on their way. We'll do all we can, Armando, and then some.''

His jaw clenched, then he nodded. ''Yes. All right. I'm out of here. Give me hourly updates, Zimmerman.'' He looked down at Laura for a long moment. Her heart went out to him. And didn't return. ''Coming, I presume?''

''You know better than to try and stop me!''

For the next weeks they worked nearly around the clock. They saved thousands and provided health care, food, drinking water, shelter and latrines to thousands more left homeless by the worst flooding to hit Argentina in over thirty years. By the end of three weeks, most people had ventured back to their homes.

Then another low pressure weather system hit.

No one was ready for the second and much worse flood wave. ''This is endless, worse—pointless!''

Laura heard Jason's mutterings. She was sure everyone did, and agreed. The bile of futility filled her up, as it must everyone else. Not only had all their work been undone, conditions were far worse now.

They were back at the flooded river's bank, one of the dozens of rescue teams, organizing another rescue operation, with no end in sight.

''Where's that rope, Romero?''

Her head snapped around to Armando's growl into his walkie-talkie. He stood there, supreme, tireless, getting the impossible done. He'd known what to do, where to go and when to get maximum results, to save the most people. She now knew why he always took over. She'd let him this time, without a word.

But no one could prevail against the merciless powers of nature.

''Romero, are you reading me?''

Romero's answer crackled at the same moment they heard the helicopter's approach. They all rushed to the driest spot around, where Romero would throw down the ropes.

In the last hours, La Clínica's and GAO's helicopters had rescued around four thousand people. But the pilots had to put them on the ground too close to the rising water, dropping them sooner so they could make more trips. The rescued had to be moved again and trucks had to risk coming close enough to take them further north. But nothing seemed enough. More and more people were in danger.

Other people reached dry land on their own. Some were too exhausted to move further and the flood water caught up with them. Many didn't understand that the water was still rising. But the most heart-rending were parents who'd lost children and wouldn't leave, tried to go back. They had to force them onto the trucks so they could take them to safety.

It was a complete disaster. The water level had risen by five meters in the past two hours. Panic was as devastating as the flood itself. In desperation, people kept trying to cross the river, only to be swept away. Finally, Laura had come up with the idea of putting sturdy ropes across the main road so people would have something to hold onto and pull their way across. Some people managed, others didn't.

This was the last rope they'd place before heading out in boats to fish out the people who'd slipped through their improvised net.

Getting the ropes slung across had been a tremendous problem. Usually the river was about three hundred meters at its widest, now it was three kilometers in places. They had to find the narrowest parts to place their ropes across, but by the time they'd devised the ropes the river had widened even more. Then came crossing the raging waters and finding something to tie it to on the other side.

As they struggled with the thick ropes, knotting ends together securely to make them as long as possible, Armando reached out to her, brushed her fringe from her eyes, cupped her cheek. He didn't say anything. His eyes did. *Tell me. Are you OK? Don't lie.*

Her answer was one fierce kiss into his palm.

They kept on working.

Four hours later, Laura snapped her eyes back from her watch to find Armando's boat moving away from hers. A frantic cry for him to come back, to stay close almost escaped. How ridiculous could she get? He had to go back. His boat was filled to overflowing and he had to deposit the people they'd saved on dry land.

Her team and Armando's had been battling against the raging waters, fishing people out, delivering them to the trucks waiting to take them to shelters, refueling then hopping back into the boats to repeat the process over and over and over again. They'd saved hundreds, performed successful CPR on dozens of near-drowning victims, but the death toll was rising.

And it was the first time their teams had been separated. Out of necessity, she knew. Still, oppressive dread numbed her. Maybe they should follow suit. Her team was soaked and exhausted. They had to have a break.

Their boat was approaching a rooftop with about three dozen screaming people on top. They had room for six or so more people. But how to convince the rest to stay put until they came back for them? With the nearly submerged roof, not to mention their own weak Spanish, it might be impossible to make a case for restraint. Maybe they should wait for Armando's team to join them.

She heard Mark's curse as he lost control over the boat in the heaving current. Then they collided with the roof and it was too late.

"Where's Laura's team?"

Constanza's question went through Armando's brain, disintegrating more of his control. He didn't need her to point out that Laura and her boat were nowhere in sight. On their last return to the river, it had been the first thing he'd noticed. He'd been fighting against his rising panic, trying to believe they'd soon reappear.

They didn't.

Sick electricity arced through him. Quite a novel feeling, nausea. At least his stomach was empty.

He hauled up two more children and their mother out of the water. Then another body swept by them as they struggled against the current.

A woman—long, dark hair… He knew nothing more.

"*Armando!*"

Armando felt cold water closing its irresistible grip around his uncoordinated body, heard Arsenio's cry as he reached the woman, his trembling hands clutching her, raising her face out of the water.

Not Laura—not Laura…

She might still be the next one to float by…

He retched. Water filled his mouth, blackness his eyes, desperation his soul. Fingers dug into his flesh, dragging him out, Spanish curses and labored breathing filling his ears.

"*Por Dios*, Armando, what came over you?" Arsenio growled. "That woman was clearly dead!"

"Laura…"

"Don't even think it, *amigo*. Your bride is a tough woman. Just remember how she's been the last weeks. Don't worry about her, she'll turn up soon."

She didn't.

They searched all day, while rescuing hundreds more people, but Laura and her team had disappeared.

Everyone tried to persuade Armando to rest, to let others take over the search, if only for a couple of hours. He'd been going non-stop for forty-eight hours. He didn't answer, wasn't sure he even heard them. *Laura, Laura, Laura* was all that filled his mind.

At last, when darkness descended, even he had to concede the futility of searching by boat. He raced to La Clínica to begin an aerial search. The only helicopter not already employed in search and rescue was *El Bicho*. As soon as he fueled and checked it, he grabbed Romero.

"You're flying *El Bicho* this time, Romero. When we find them, I'll need you to hover while I go down to them."

"Armando, it's pitch black and with all that water and *El Bicho*'s pathetic lights we won't see a thing."

Armando looked at him, not seeing him, seeing only Laura being swept away, crying out for him. Without a word he jumped into the pilot's seat and started the pre-flight procedures.

"*Por Dios*, Armando!" Romero exclaimed. "All right—just move over!"

Soon they were airborne, heading to the last place Laura and her team had been seen, going over the areas already searched, then heading downstream, where they must have been swept. Night over the ravaged areas was the unimaginable setting of a nightmare. The roar of the tumbling waters and downpour drowned even the din of the rotors. Armando heard nothing but his own stampeding heart and his frantic calls dissipating into the night.

Two futile hours later, he was still looking down on the frightening expanses of inky waters. They had swelled, engulfing lives and achievements, and would still cause untold damage long after they'd receded. Suddenly, an overpowering sensation took him over. An alien urge to give up.

Just jump in and join Laura, the waters urged.

He jerked away from the edge. *No.* It *wouldn't* end this way. Not for either of them. Laura was a survivor, a fighter, resourceful, sharp, fearless. She was keeping her team together, keeping them safe, until he came for her. She'd know he'd never give up on her.

His hand burned with the imprint of her kiss. He pressed it to his lips and tasted her again.

He whispered to her, let the elements carry his pledge: "I'm coming for you, *mi corazón.*"

"Did you hear that?"

Susan, Jason and Mark jerked their heads up at Laura's eager question, listened—then turned to her.

"Hear what?" Susan grumbled, suppressing another violent shudder.

Mark tightened his arm around her. "Besides the torrent's noise and the cries for help, you mean?" he huffed, his teeth chattering too.

"Maybe she means the helicopters that keep missing us by miles!" Jason added sourly, adjusting his cramped position on the thick branch they were all trapped on. "Missing us? Sorry, as if they could ever see us under this foliage!"

"Don't mind me," Laura mumbled, and they huddled closer together again, fighting against exposure and exhaustion. They'd drift away and drown if they succumbed.

So they hadn't heard. Only she had. Armando, calling to her...

OK, she couldn't have. Especially since she'd heard him whispering. She was probably hallucinating with exhaustion and hypothermia. That would explain how she could *feel* him, out there somewhere, looking for her. Determined, unstoppable.

Or maybe it was having his blood in her veins! She was getting fanciful here, but maybe, just maybe, it had forged some kind of link between them. One fifth of the blood keeping her heart beating was his, transfused into her after her accident, saving her—yet again.

And he'd never mentioned it. It took the long night of sitting stranded in this tree, half in, half out of the roiling waters, for her teammates to tell her. They'd mentioned it in passing, just another thing to take their minds off their predicament.

Not that it was possible. All she could see in the pitch darkness was a replay of the heart-bursting moments when their boat had overturned under too many people fighting to climb onto it. Once floundering in the water, it had been all she could do to strike out after a long piece of rope. She'd thrown it to the others so they'd at least stay together. Then they'd drifted endlessly, ending up clinging to the same tree. Her plan wasn't much. At dawn, they'd try to swim to a rooftop where maybe Armando and the others would end up seeing them.

Now they waited. At least the waters had stopped rising.

But the night was endless. And the helicopters had stopped circling.

Had they given up on them?

No. Armando, her protector—he'd *never* give up.

Armando was in the air again the second that night gave the slightest way to dawn. The hour when he'd had to relinquish his search to refuel had almost destroyed his sanity. People had parted at his advance as if from the path of another impending disaster.

Was this how loving someone unhinged you, wrecked you, while at the same time making you invincible?

"All right, Armando," Romero shouted to him over the combined cacophony of the helicopter and the flood waters. "What's the search plan now?"

"The same as before. They must have searched for anything jutting above water to hang onto."

"There was nothing of the sort for thirty miles from the point you last saw them."

"Then they must have drifted further. We'll keep going even if we have to follow the river to the ocean!"

Romero's look of pitying disbelief made it clear he thought this a deluded hope. Fighting the urge to knock the expression off with his fist, Armando growled, "We're not stopping until we find them. Do you understand, Romero?"

Romero's eyes widened, then, without even a nod, he turned his attention to flying the helicopter.

Get a grip, Salazar, Armando berated himself. *He's on your side. Now concentrate. Look for signs of life.*

They found plenty among the devastation. But not Laura or any of her team. They rescued all they could, until there was no more room. Those people had to be flown to dry land before they could come back for more.

No way was he putting off his search that long now!

"Romero, fly over to that factory," he shouted. "Set me down on the roof. I'm taking the inflatable boat. Come back for me in an hour."

"What if you go missing, too?"

"I won't."

He barely heard Romero's shouted protest as he threw the bundled boat out of the helicopter then jumped out after it, landing on his side with jarring force.

As soon as the rotors' draft relented, he pounced on the boat, inflated it. In minutes he was tying himself to it, pushing it over the roof, the five meters' drop to the water surface a weird disembodied feeling, followed by a too-solid impact.

He landed on the same side again. Something felt torn. *Forget it.*

He started paddling, trying to gain some control over the boat, passing by many rooftops with people trapped on top. *Laura—find Laura.* Those people were not in immediate danger. Others would come for them.

He stopped rowing. The current was so strong, he had no need to row. If Laura had drifted at that speed for an hour, she should be around here. But where—*where*?

Suddenly, something red caught his eye. Something in the distance—over in a tree? His heart almost kicked its way out of his ribcage. Laura had been wearing red.

A sign!

A bout of inhuman strength rode him as he maneuvered the boat towards the tree. But—was it a sign, or had it been torn off her?

"Laura!" His shout drowned even the water's roar as he neared.

Dios, Dios, let it be a sign…

The thick foliage shook and an arm emerged, waved—a supple, feminine arm. *Laura!*

Rain poured down, but now it was painful, scalding his eyes, blurring them. And then it wasn't raining any more. It made no sense. But all he cared about was that he'd found her. *Found her.* Alive.

Debilitating relief turned to panic. He was going too fast. He'd overtake them! *No*—no, he wouldn't. He defied the current, moving the boat diagonally. As he neared the tree, he could now see both Laura's head and Jason's sticking out of it. What were they shouting?

"Laura, I'm coming!"

From a hundred meters away, he finally made out her screams. "No, no! The branches will rupture the boat. Keep away!"

His mind stalled. How *could* he keep away?

But if he didn't, all he'd manage would be to join them in

that tree. Romero would come back to find the bright orange boat more shredded flotsam!

"Then jump!" he bellowed.

"No!" Laura screamed again. "You pass us by—we'll jump in after you."

Of course. If they jumped first he would have to chase after them, might be unable to catch them, or catch them all. This way he'd paddle against the current to slow himself down until they reached him and scrambled aboard.

In minutes Mark was the first to reach him. Armando helped him into the boat—but Laura... She was sweeping by the boat—slipping away... "No! *Laura!*"

His heart burst. Then Jason was pulling himself on board and Armando noticed the rope connecting them.

She *had* kept them together. This just *had* to be her doing! Laura and her rope ideas...

At last she was out of the water, in his arms, shuddering, cold, limp and half-naked. All the strength holding him together ebbed. He joined the others in their collapse, flat on his back with her on top of him.

Safe. She was safe. In his arms. Everything else ceased to matter.

From another dimension he heard then saw Romero's helicopter approaching, saw her bloodless face filling his vision, heard her wobbly words, couldn't make them out. Suddenly he was back in full focus, panic flooding his system again. What if it wasn't only exposure and exhaustion? What if she was injured? Too hurt to speak?

"What, *mi corazón*?" he gasped. "Are you OK? Are you hurt?"

She shook her head, her tremulous smile penetrating him with love and relief. "I just said this is one hell of a honeymoon!"

CHAPTER EIGHT

"You realize you're in my lair, don't you?"

Armando smiled as he closed the door behind him, that smile that made hormones roar in her system. Made her wonder how long she'd be able to keep from pouncing on him and tearing his clothes off.

"Yes, Lion King!"

His smile widened at her teasing reply, and she sighed in bone-deep delight. Earning his smiles had become a cause, an aspiration. So this was how it felt to crave, to find wonder and glory in being alive, no matter what life threw at her—just because he existed.

"Are you telling me something, *mi corazón*?"

She pressed her hand to her heart. Being called *his*, so playfully yet with those obsidian eyes so intense, so sincere...

She shifted with restless hope, tucking her feet beneath her, resting on one arm and letting her head fall to one side. Her newly washed hair cascaded across her sensitized back. Just his presence turned every move into something erotic, every contact with her own clothes into arousal.

"Only that yours is the only room that doesn't have twenty-plus people in it," she said, weaving her fingers into her hair, her hypersensitive senses quivering with even her own touch. "Señora Amarilli had locked it, refusing to let anyone in..."

"Anyone but the lion's lady. Well, Señora Leóna, excuse the weary king of the jungle as he indulges in some long overdue grooming."

A wink and a feather touch on the tip of her nose doused her in another wave of longing, more sweeping than the flood had been. She really had to do something about her condition.

125

Tearing his clothes off would be good for a start, then hers, then…

A dozen feet stamped down the corridor outside, jerking her out of her erotic haze.

The house was still swarming with people, those who'd yet to find a shelter or return to their homes. So many had had their homes destroyed. So much suffering had been endured, and would still be endured for a long time to come. Shouldn't she be ashamed of having those totally selfish, hedonistic thoughts in these conditions?

Well, she wasn't. They were doing everything they could to help—rebuilding homes, rehabilitating the injured and the bereaved, restoring order. In her own mind and heart she was entitled to her own compartment of joy, untouched by anything else. And that compartment was full of him.

She resumed the pleasure of watching him, savoring the heavy ache in her heart and loins. He turned, taking off his shoes, stretching. Just his movement about the room was pure poetry, his every move the essence of unconscious grace and innate power. He radiated life and vitality. It was no wonder the three nights back home without him had felt lifeless, even with the place overflowing with people. The three nights he'd sent her home, telling her he'd follow, then hadn't.

This, at last, was his first night home since that day two weeks ago when he'd dragged her and her team out of the flood.

That day, he'd insisted she and her team recuperate from their ordeal for as long as possible. They'd insisted a day was enough. He'd been adamant that Laura at least should come in from then on for a regular day shift—no night shifts, no field missions. He'd only succeeded in getting her to rest one more day, then she'd been back on full time, matching him hour for hour.

By the end of the first week, he'd given up. His ultra-intensity, that obsession with keeping her under his observation and away from danger, had seemed to switch off. Then another switch had flicked on, full force. Another sort of intensity. Erotic, seductive, maddening. But from afar. Just looks, whispers, innuendo. Not one touch, not one attempt. He had left her in no doubt he wanted her, yet had left it up to her to make the first move. Damn him!

Now that first move was all she could think of making. She wanted him. How she wanted him. She wanted their marriage to be real, as real as he cared to make it. How real that would be, she had no idea.

Not that she cared any more. She'd taken him for her husband. Now she was taking him, all the way.

Armando watched her uncoiling herself off the bed, coming towards him.

The way his body and senses rioted, he knew he should grab a change of clothes and run for his couch in La Clínica. He turned, escaping her, entered the bathroom, busied himself with shaving.

By now he was almost grateful for the flood. It had gotten him through the last five weeks, distracting him, depleting him…

And who was he kidding? He was neither distracted nor depleted. His focus on her, ever since he'd thought he'd lost her, had been like a spear lodged inside his brain. A spear that kept twisting inside him with every mixed signal she gave.

One moment he thought she wanted him, or was at least wavering, so he encouraged her, opened up. The next she was opaque, making him stumble back, losing any ground he thought he'd gained.

The temptation to drag her, give her no choice, seduce her out of her inhibitions and reservations was overpowering. But now, besides needing her to need him of her own free will, to need him for real, another thing stopped him.

Diego's memory. Respect for it had to be behind her ambivalence. *He* had to respect that. Not that respecting it made it more bearable.

More bearable? It was *un*bearable. He could take a lot, but he'd reached his limit. By the time she thought it right to live and love again, he might be in an asylum.

End it now. She's hurt you enough. Your fault, sure, but it isn't any less damaging.

"Laura…"

"Armando…"

"You first," he rasped. The words "Let's have an annulment" froze on his lips at the look in her eyes. Was she finally going to act on her hunger?

She wet her lips. "Do you, uh, have the latest figures in damage estimates?"

Hah! What a fool! Falling into the same trap over and over again.

He bent his head to the basin, removing excess foam and splashing his face with hot water, trying to make the actions quell his agitation, his disappointment.

He straightened, avoided her eyes in the mirror. "It's staggering. Apart from human and property losses, Santa Fe province is one of Argentina's most important agricultural regions. The flooded lands have not only had their crops destroyed, they won't be cultivatable for years. Authorities estimate the flooding will cost farmers at least five hundred million dollars."

Her lips made a silent, pained "Oh." Her eyes went dark olive with anguish and regret. How had he ever thought her a superficial media darling? Why did she have to prove him so wrong? He'd wanted her enough even believing the worst of her. Now—now…

Now he had to get out of here.

Coward! Dumb, stupid, pathetic coward! Laura's vicious inner critic was lavish with name-calling as usual. Armando was turning away, gathering his clothes. He was leaving her again.

She was damned if she'd let him, if she'd keep their relationship frozen in this limbo!

Another voice, that of her insecurities and fears, made itself heard. *But maybe he's walking away because it doesn't really make a difference to him. He'd like you in his bed, but only if you fall into it. He isn't even willing to reach out and give you a little nudge.*

Well, she didn't need a little nudge! She'd been ready, eager, breathless since...since she'd first seen him?

Oh, Lord! Was that what all those chaotic feelings towards him had been? If this was true then she'd...

Not now—cross-examine yourself later! He's opening the door, saying goodbye. Stop him!

"You haven't showered."

Lame, lame, *lame*! This was all she could come up with?

It was clear he thought so, too. He didn't even fully turn as he said, "I've freshened up. We should contribute to fresh water conservation in our crisis."

"It doesn't have to be a running shower. Half a tub and..." Her eyes clung to his movements as he rubbed the side of his neck then down and back between his shoulder-blades. He'd been doing that since he'd thrown himself off a roof to save her. "And you look like you could really use a massage!"

He frowned.

That hadn't been in the script. Definitely not the reaction she'd expected to her seduction efforts, blundering as they were. Well, no matter. She was seducing him, with or without his co-operation.

She pushed the door closed, took his hand and led him back into the room.

"Bath or massage first?"

He went still as he looked down on her, so beautiful he made everything inside her quiver, his expression too complex to fathom. Not making it easy, was he? Fine. She never cared for easy. And she'd certainly come to the right man for hard and challenging.

Her fingers strayed over him, indulged in what they'd been on fire for all her life. His stopped them as they undid his shirt, slipped it over one shoulder.

He still wore that strange neutral expression. ''Are you still feeling bad about my neck strain?'' he rasped.

OK. So he might not be as bright as she'd thought he was after all.

''It's an *injury*, and you got it saving me—again.'' She started kneading his neck. He let her do it for a moment, then removed her hand again, a stiff smile on his lips.

''Don't tire your little hands, *querida*.''

''My little hands are tougher than they look—and very clever, too!''

Onyx eyes locked on hers, the slant more pronounced, their influence, their beauty deepening. And what was that raw gleam? Uncertainty? Oh, my. He'd better be asking what she thought he was.

She'd give him her answer anyway!

''If you're having a tough time deciding between bath and massage, I'll give you both at the same time.''

Armando closed his eyes.

Was she out to kill him?

Did she really want him, or did she just think it time to become a real wife to him? He knew her now. She had that ridiculous sense of duty. And along with that dangerous gratitude she'd been accumulating since the day of her accident... She'd been very vocal about it since she'd learned of the blood transfusion, since that day in the flood. More so when she'd discovered he'd ruptured a muscle then. Duty, gratitude and, worst of all, pity. And if it wasn't only over his injury, but because she'd realized how he felt about her—that would be unendurable.

He opened his eyes to the feel of her hands on him again, removing his shirt halfway down his arms. He groaned, suppressing the quake that swept him into a shudder.

Grab her. She's offering herself, so just take her. Throw her on that bed, or trap her against that wall, and just bury yourself in her. Before you have a stroke!

He couldn't. Even if it did kill him, he had to let it be her choice.

But this is her choice now.

No. Not until he was certain why she was making it.

"I would appreciate some help here." She tugged at him again, still not having much effect. "Unlocking your gears would do for a start."

A smile bubbled up in spite of his turmoil. "And then? You intend to release me from my shackles?" He looked at where his arms were strapped to his chest by his half-opened shirt.

"Oh, I will—unless you go for such things!"

He had to laugh. Her sense of humor tickled him, no matter where or what. He let her lead him to the bed. "I should have known you'd be into bondage, you and your rope fetish."

"A rope gets the job done. But now that you mention it— ah! The possibilities!" She turned up a radiant face to him and completed unbuttoning his shirt. *Dios*, her beauty, the translucency of her skin, her eyes—her spirit. She looked happy now. Truly happy. For him? Dared he believe?

He let her push him down onto the bed, his heart slowing down, each beat rocking him. She came up behind him on the bed, a deliberate rub against him bringing her kneeling at his back, her knees on either side of his hips. Then his shirt was sliding down his back, her hands accompanying it in one languorous sweep.

She *was* out to kill him.

On their way back up, her fingers changed purpose and pressure. The feathering that had nearly finished him became exploratory gliding then greedy kneading. Twisting in his hair, burying in his congealing muscles, tapping into his screaming-pitch tension, draining it, feeding it.

He no longer knew where the tremors originated—her fingers or his every nerve and muscle. Or the moans—were they pushing their aroused, agonized way out of her throat or his?

"Your hands…very…clever…indeed…" he gasped as she

dipped her fingers into the exact spots of hurt, relieved them, spread comfort into the burning flesh, inflicted a worse agony.

"Wait till you feel what my lips can do!" She breathed her hot promise into his neck, then made good on it instantly. He almost went over the edge there and then. He did go over the edge of his reticence, his fear of having his fears confirmed. He just had to know.

He threw his head back, snared her eyes in his, groaned, "Why?"

So actions *didn't* speak louder than words, huh? That luscious man demanded those, too. And he'd have them. Oh, yes…

"Because I'll burst or burn or worse if I don't. I want you— want you—*want* you…" A more daring caress and kiss kept rhythm with her words, then she hugged him from the back, squashed herself against him. "I'll also die if I don't get my hands and lips all over you, pamper you, unwind you. Help me, you big man!"

He helped her then, moving into whatever position she was urging him into, ending up sprawled on the bed, face down.

His back was rising and falling as fast as her chest, his voice as unsteady as hers. "If this is unwinding me, I'd hate to see what you'll do when you want to drive me crazy. I don't think I'd survive it."

She heard a giddy laugh, an uninhibited sound of elation and expectation. Was it hers? Was that *her*? Wanton, audacious and proud? Was that how hunger transformed when it was at last unleashed?

She mounted him, opening her knees wide to encompass his body, positioning herself to give him the most thorough massage imaginable. But the moment she had his steel hips between her legs, she found herself pressing down on his jeans-covered flesh to assuage the searing ache there, if only momentarily. He jerked up on a feral growl, grinding himself back into her, trying to turn.

She threw herself over his back to hamper him, bit his ear,

gasped in it, "Not yet…please, darling…" His jerk was more violent this time, his groan pained. She buried deep, moist, biting kisses along his jaw, his neck. "Let me indulge myself—indulge you…"

His teeth didn't even unclench to deliver the staccato words. "You'd better indulge yourself fast—you're killing me, not indulging me…"

Her laugh was pure wickedness this time, elemental feminine power flooding her, never tasted and instantly addictive. "You're invulnerable, remember, Dr. Salazar, alias Superman? You'll survive…"

Armando was beginning to doubt this seriously. Surely he'd overload any second now? His nervous system couldn't possibly withstand that level of stimulation for much longer before it burnt out! He lay under her, giving her free rein with his body, face down, eyes closed, his body shaking apart, his senses far into the red zone. He'd almost seized when she'd called him darling!

Maybe he was dreaming again. Worse, maybe he'd snapped! He'd wanted her too long, too intensely. Delusions might now be giving him his heart's desire.

She bit his deltoid. Her fingers and lips and tongue gave him no respite, rampaging all over him. Her moist heat singed his hips through both their clothes. He writhed, panted, spiking to a higher plateau of arousal.

No, no—this *had* to be real. He'd never imagined anything like this from her, anything like this happening to him. No fantasy, no delusion could reach this, could do this to him.

The firm softness of her breasts pressed against his back again through her nightgown as she leaned over him, her hot thighs trembling as she braced herself just off him, then her hands dipped beneath his waist, urging him up so she could reach his jeans fastening. It was her words that broke him.

"Oh, God, Armando, I've starved for you. Nothing should be so beautiful. I want the rest of you…"

"Enough!" He erupted into motion, pulling her beneath him, bearing down on her, thrusting at her, blind, out of his mind.

Her surrender was instant, melting into him, feeding his frenzy.

"Armando, *please...*"

The ragged whisper penetrated his ferocious haze. He jerked away from her. "What? I hurt you...?"

"No, no. I just want—*need* to bathe you! I haven't been sleeping with fantasizing about gliding my hands all over you, slick in lather... Oh-h!"

She was in the air, in his arms, and in the bathroom in seconds. He only put her down to start filling the tub, then turned on her again, his mouth crashing down on hers, lifting her high against the wall, spreading her thighs around his waist. Just like that time in the riot, only this time—oh, this time... Her mind sputtered, stopped.

"Share your fantasies with me, always...." He broke off to thrust against her, keeping the rhythm with his tongue in her mouth. "Just not now—I can't take it now..."

She grabbed at his maddening tongue, suckled it hard, another gush of pure madness flooding her. "You said plenty of hot, hard sex, didn't you?" she gasped. "As in encores? As many as possible for each fantasy...?"

He eased her to the floor. "No more, *amada*. No more torment!"

She had no time to object. Virtuoso hands had her down to her panties in a second. Then her breasts were his. One in his palm, one in his mouth. Becoming instruments of pleasure he played to unbearable pitches. Sensations battered their way out of her throat. Her strength gave way to his, giving him total surrender. His enslaving voice reverberated in her flesh. "*Mi corazón—te quiero—te quiero tanto mi amor...*"

Suddenly the lips that had been drawing hard on her nipples melted down her burning flesh, everywhere, until she felt devoured, finished—exquisite. His tongue ended where all tension converged, opened her, tasted her readiness. And without warning, over-stimulation mushroomed outwards. She screamed, convulsed, ecstasy destroying her, re-creating her…

Time slowed, then disappeared. She was no more, nowhere. There was only Armando. He was there, completing her pleasure, then coming up to surround her, contain her in her aftermath.

Laura no longer knew anything. She'd thought she'd known physical gratification. So what was that? Maybe he'd know. "Uh…uh…what happened?"

"Just the best gift I ever had, *mi amor*, the most beautiful thing I ever saw, heard—*felt*." His tongue thrust now, healing, soothing, deepening the intimacy, his teeth taking gentle bites of lips that quivered with stupefaction.

She'd hungered for intimacy with him, yet hadn't equated it with finding anything like this. After Diego, she'd doubted she *could* enjoy sex. The searing peak of arousal Armando drove her to was as high as she'd hoped to reach, and she'd been content with that. She'd just wanted his closeness, all the way, every way, giving *him* pleasure!

But just one touch and she'd… She couldn't begin to describe what had happened inside her. Oh, boy. And he hadn't made her his yet! But surely nothing could be that good? No way could it be better! Maybe she'd never feel anything like that again. She suspected she'd blown some fuse permanently.

He raised his head, his gaze gentle and fierce all at once. Possessive, triumphant, yet vulnerable.

It staggered her to find that she wanted him even more now. Satiation had only brought on a fiercer hunger for him. So her fuses were still intact, maybe even just hitting their stride. But first, before she burst…

She slipped out of his slackened hold, dropping to her knees before him, giving him no time to object this time. Driven by uncanny precision and purpose, she released him.

"Laura, don't…"

Armando forgot what he was going to cry out, why. Forgot how to speak. Her wanton grasp was worshiping him, soft cheeks and lips rubbing scorching silk against him. He heard a roar. His? From afar, he heard her beloved voice, trembling, awed. "Magnificent... Oh, Armando, you're just—just, oh, darling..."

Though his mind imploded, his body tried to hold on, hold back, still demanding hers around it before it would let go. But her loving was just too much.

Crashing waves of satisfaction brought him to his knees before her, devastating tenderness demanding her in his arms, beneath his skin, at once.

His arms snatched her up, fused her to his flesh, emotions escaping him on harsh sobs. "Laura, Laura, *mi vida, mi amor...*"

Never before—he'd never known there could be this much.

Now he wanted more. Everything.

Her.

Laura clung to Armando, returning his tender ferocity, barriers dissolving between their flesh. All was sensation, emotion, no thought left. OK—only *one* thought left. How ready he still was. Oh, what was he waiting for? "Armando—*please!*"

He understood, cupped her face, passion melting his hands around it, his eyes on hers. "*Si, mi vida.* Now. At last."

He made sweeping her up seem effortless. She tasted his neck, bliss closing her eyes. He'd take her to his bed, lay her down and bear down on her, make her his. She found herself lowered on top of him instead, in water!

He chuckled in her ears, started soaping her. "That bath, remember?"

"*I'm* supposed to bathe *you*! And my fantasy was to do it in the master bedroom tub—under that skylight!" She buried her protest and lips in any part of him she could reach.

In answer, his hands closed on her breasts, slippery, hot, possessive. He suckled her neck, his hardness nudging her, opening her. "You will. You'll do everything you want, everything you can imagine, anything at all—to me, with me."

"Oh, God, Armando. Too much…" Her body arched, frustration tearing through her.

His lusty growl in her ear was a plea. "Tell me you want me again, *mi amor*. Tell me how much."

"I can't! I craved you before. Now this—there are no words…"

"*Si, si mi* Laura—no words, only this!" And he thrust into her.

Yet he still held back.

No. "Armando!"

He misunderstood her frenzy. "*Dios!* I've hurt you. I—"

"No, no—don't hold back!" She arched her hips more, begging, writhing, shameless. "All of you—have to have all of you."

He thwarted her, taking his time, easing into her in slow motion, letting her body blossom for him. When her head tossed against his shoulder, masses of hair and sensations blinding her, he withdrew—then gave her what she needed to topple over, a free fall under monstrous gravity. She cried out, cried, until she could cry no more, convulse no more, fell apart.

"Again!" He moved again, picking up speed.

"Can't…"

"*Si, mi amor, si*—you can, again, and again. A promise is a promise." His fingers fondled her, stroking her, stoking her inside and out. Soon she was whimpering and begging again. He slowed down. Picked up speed again, then slowed again. He waited until desperation had depleted her, then brought her to another climax.

Enervated, she still struggled for enough awareness to revel in his own release, in that final plunge that had him calling out to her his agonized ecstasy, pouring himself into her. Then she shut down.

She came to herself again as he was laying her down on his bed, semi-dry, quivering with aftershocks. Her worshiping eyes clung to him as he flung the window open, letting in the jasmine-laden breeze. Then he came back to love her again.

Everything had changed.

Her heart beat to a different rhythm, her skin had a richer texture, colors had magical hues and life tasted and smelled of him...Armando!

He was there, beside her, all around her. Passion, mastery and tenderness made human. Made male. All male. And he'd made her all woman, all beautiful, all desirable. With just a look, a touch. He just had to be around—and she was all alive. For the first time in her life.

Her eyes on him woke him just as his on her had all through the night. Alert, insatiable eyes reclaimed her. "Armando!"

He didn't need more than that wavering plea, coming over her, his full weight ecstasy, security—necessity.

No preliminaries this time. No words either. They'd poured all their passion out before. This time all endearments were transmitted through their locked gazes as he moved inside her, not touching her except for conquering her, surrendering to her. It grew too fierce, too quickly. She capitulated under the brutal onslaught of pleasure, closed her eyes. He wouldn't let her.

"Open your eyes, *mi vida*." His growl reverberated in her, peremptory, pleading. "See what you do to me. Let me see what I do to you."

She obeyed, saw it all, let him see it all.

Her hands dug into mahogany silk and copper flesh, as her body wept for him, dragged him with her into the abyss of satiation.

You're not giving me a chance. Diego was screaming at her again.

She surfaced just enough to realize she was dreaming. A dream tinged with guilty memories, in taxation for so much bliss, it seemed.

Poor Diego. It had taken loving Armando to make her realize she'd done far worse than that. She'd given him nothing. Then he'd died.

Armando stirred. a sixth sense telling him that she had at least turned in her sleep. Then he heard her moan, ''Oh, Diego!'' as if her heart was breaking.

His did.

CHAPTER NINE

"DIEGO would have loved this, don't you think?"

Give it a few seconds, Armando ordered himself.

He needed them to curb the cutting reply inside him, slashing him to pieces. The bustle of the technicians installing the magnetic resonance imaging machine bought him more time.

"He just loved high-tech gadgets," Laura went on. He braced himself against her euphoric smile, her excited squeeze on his arm. "He would have loved seeing La Clínica being equipped to the hilt!"

He opened his mouth, ready to make some evasive answer, then closed it again on a resigned sigh. She'd turned to the technicians, directing them in the instrument's placement.

She didn't want, didn't expect an answer. Just more rhetoric—again. And again. And *again*. Diego this. Diego that. She'd almost never mentioned him before, but now—now he was always on her lips. Clearly always on her mind.

Always in her heart?

And he'd thought it unbearable before!

But how could it be? It made no sense.

Diego *had* been like a younger brother to him, a fact of life, an insoluble blood tie. He'd once loved the very young Diego. But love hadn't weathered the changes—in him, in Diego. It had turned to fond tolerance. Then there'd been times when even that had run out, when aggravation and disappointment had taken over. Then there had been Laura, and he'd known any relationship could outlast its warranty. Soft feelings lingered, better times, worthier traits echoed, but...

There had come a time when he'd wished Diego gone. Then Diego *had* gone and he'd wished him back. He still mourned him. Mourned the loss of memories, the waste of potential, missed even the warts. But that was him, loving a relative even knowing his faults all too well. What explained Laura's attachment?

It really made no sense. Blind sentiment was for lesser women, weaker individuals. He'd known her more than five months now, half of which she'd been his indispensable colleague and co-director. And she'd been his wife for real, his insatiable lover, for a month.

He'd not only plundered her body and sated himself on her passion, he'd studied her, analyzed her faculties and probed her mind. It didn't add up that a woman so astute, so critical, so demanding, both personally and professionally, could have fallen for Diego in the first place, not to mention still holding a candle for him now.

But she is, Salazar, that knife-twisting voice inside him taunted. *Eat your heart out.*

And he was. How he was.

"Ooh, this is perfect, isn't it?" Laura launched herself at him, almost jumping up and down. "All that remains are the lab lists and the new surgical microscopes and La Clínica will be the best equipped medical center in Argentina!"

He didn't answer.

Her eyes dimmed. "What?"

"Nothing. It's great to have an MRI scanner."

"But?"

"There's no but."

"Oh, yes, there is. Out with it, Salazar!"

For answer, he just rushed her out of the room. "Arsenio, you take care of installation and any signatures in our stead, OK?'

"Sure. Where's the fire?"

"Hey, where're we going?"

His friend's teasing and Laura's protest canceled each other out. He didn't attempt to answer either or even slow down.

The two dozen strides to one of La Clínica's many storage

rooms were punctuated by her spluttering chuckles. He opened it, dragged her inside, turned on her.

"A word of caution, you edible man. That door opens to the outside."

"Even if I hadn't put it there myself, I just opened it. " He advanced on her. She retreated. At least her feet did. Her eyes—they were already ripping him out of his clothes.

"So what happens if someone opens it?"

"Then they get more than they came here intending to find."

"You really go that extra mile for your people's morale, don't you?" She let him haul her to him, melting in his grasp, her breathing already catching, the scent of her instant arousal intoxicating. "Nothing's too steep to provide them with free entertainment, huh?"

"It isn't free." Her white coat fell to the floor, her shirt parted beneath his anxious fingers, yanked out of her elasticated-waist pants. Then those and her panties followed her coat. At twenty weeks her pregnancy was still only apparent when she was naked, though her thickening waist had long demanded the extra leeway. "*You're* paying, *mi amor*. You called me Salazar. You know what happens when you call me Salazar."

"Ooh, menacing! Love it. But it happens when I call you anything—and when I don't— Oh-h…"

His lips closed on one nipple. Her breasts… He couldn't get enough of them, getting riper, giving her more pleasure when he freed them, captured them. He bent her over a damaged trolley, tore open his shirt, writhing his hair-roughened chest against them. Her moans answered his, her legs bent, braced at the edge, desperate for anything he did to her. He reached shaking fingers to probe her, found her molten.

He had that at least. Had her out of her mind, addicted, totally at his mercy.

Just like she had him.

Dragging her pants all the way down had been easy. Not

so his, not with the obstacle of his arousal and her frantic hands fighting his for access to it.

"Laura, stop!"

"I said out with it Salazar. Didn't know how prophetic I was…' Her chuckle ended on a frenzied moan as she rubbed against him. He stilled her movements.

"Payback is getting bigger, *amor*…" he panted

"Oh, yes, it is!" she gasped, massaging him, grabbing at him. "Oh, please…"

Two buttonholes of his fly ripped under his frenzied fingers. She dragged him, then he was all the way inside her.

New, every time. More, better, always. She gave all of herself—or was it only all of her passion, her body…? *Love you. Need you. You!* Confessing, begging—on every lunge into her flesh. Giving her, giving in to her. Could it be she didn't understand? The words he was muttering in his mother tongue? Or their reality?

"Armando—*Armando*…" Her cries stifled. His answering groans did, too, as he succumbed to ecstasy almost damaging in its intensity.

She lay back, filled with him, with all he gave, delirious in the aftermath. His hands swept her, committing more precious freedoms to memory, to soul, passing by her belly. Swelling, but not with his love, his seed. Was that pain survivable?

Then he felt it.

Something jerked her out of her sated stupor. Her eyes flew to him, found shock much larger than hers in his ebony eyes, then swerved to where their bodies were still meshed. Another flutter crinkled beneath her skin.

He jackknifed out of her as if he'd been shot. "What…?"

Rising to her elbows, she reached for him, anxious for his anxiety.

"*Dios*…" was all he could say as he staggered back, his hands fumbling with his clothes.

She put on her clothes with trembling hands, too. The baby

had moved for the first time. It should have mattered. Only Armando's shock did.

"It's just the baby, darling!"

"*Just* the baby? *Dios!* It's because I... Too hard. *Por Dios*—what an animal!"

All consternation fled. The wonderful, indescribable man! He thought he'd hurt her, hurt the baby. "Oh, yes—what a prime, magnificent animal. Stupid, too. It's time the baby started moving, that's all, darling."

"You sure?"

"You a doctor?"

"Right now? No. I'm flabbergasted!"

She threw her arms around him, squeezed with all she had. "You make one awesome flabbergasted. No flabber in any form or quantity anywhere, though."

"You're fine? Sure? And the baby...?"

"I can't possibly be better and survive it. The baby was just saying hello."

His eyes closed, his arms too, around her, his forehead dropping to hers, pressing, rubbing. Her lungs filled with his agitated breathing, her heart with his tremors. It awed her, humbled her to have all that caring, all that tenderness from such power, such toughness. And what she felt in return...

Their beepers went off. His head snapped up, his hand too.

"*Madre de Dios*, we've been here an hour!"

"No way!"

"I guess Arsenio thought it enough time to put out any fire."

Laura giggled, fierce delight flooding her at his return to lightness. "Not our kind of fire!"

"No." His eyes said the rest, all the stormy endearments and promises. "Let's get work out of the way first."

Outside, grinning faces met them as they took the stairs to ER.

"Why do I get the feeling they're not just greeting us?"

she said, her hands going to her braid, her clothes. Everything was back in place. She hoped.

"Because they aren't. They're onto us." His easy words changed into chuckling as he looked sideways at her. "*Mi* Laura! Your blushing blows me away. So glorious, yet so strange, coming from you."

"You saying I'm shameless?"

"Oh, yes. To my eternal gratitude!"

"*Later*, Salazar!" He gave a gracious bow, accepting the sensual threat, his eyes making his own. But something still lingered there, something…subdued. His scare over her and the baby, or something else? She remembered the reticence that had started all that, had to ask. "You haven't told me your objections to getting the MRI yet."

He was going to deny he had any. She knew him, the man she loved more than life. She could also see the moment his mind turned, and he decided to tell her.

"Having an MRI is great, but I wish you could have persuaded your benefactors to give us cash instead. Its price could have equipped a dozen clinics with every sort of less specialized but more widely used instruments and devices—all kinds of surgical instruments, X-ray machines, oximeters, cardiac monitors, even a few dialysis machines!"

"If you think I could've done that then maybe you didn't get all the details! The donation was specifically made for one exorbitant piece of medical technology. They even dictated the manufacturer! The whole thing had a load of legal mumbo-jumbo attached to it. I would've wasted months haggling, maybe even losing the grant altogether. There are plenty of other establishments out there who aren't about to look a gift horse in the mouth!"

"I'm just saying I wished we'd had our pick. But I wish for so many things that are never coming true."

What was that deadening in his eyes, in his voice? Was it just professional disappointment, or was it directed towards her? Had she failed him somehow? She had no idea.

Oppression, thick and sudden, turned everything gray. She had to say something, defend everything. "We did get the vaccines to cover Santa Fe after the flood, water sanitation is almost back to normal, and GAO's intervention is speeding up the rebuilding. I know in the situation an MRI sounds like a superfluous luxury but—"

He snapped her a quick denying glance as they ran when their pagers went off again. "*Querida*, I'm in no way implying that this isn't welcome or that you didn't do a magnificent job."

"Just as long as you believe that I couldn't have dictated terms, couldn't have asked for alternatives, even if the grant came from a foundation that carries my father's name!"

They'd reached the ER. Before he pushed the door open, he stopped her, cupped her cheek. "Of course I believe you, *amada*. Implicitly!"

"Oh!" He did? "I…" No words came. None were enough. She dragged his head down to hers, her lips a fierce press of gratitude on his. He was still hard with need for her. Only fair. She was still molten…

"Later, Laura Salazar," he groaned.

The ER was crammed as usual, but it didn't look like anyone needed them. Constanza and Arsenio, as well as Susan, Mark and Jason, ran in too, none of them having any idea why they'd been paged.

Lucianna came running in after them, giving them a rundown of the situation. "A bridge collapsed—it was damaged in the floods but seemed to be holding up and was reopened. Many cars fell off into the river, including a school bus."

"*Dios!* We're never going to see the end of the damage that flood caused!" Constanza groaned.

"Are casualties coming in, or are we going out to get them?" Armando rapped out the question.

"That's the dilemma. Many are already on their way here. People jumped in and rescued them and are driving them over.

But many are still either trapped in their vehicles or have just been dragged to the banks.''

"We'll split up, then. Half will take care of incoming casualties, while the rest head to the scene of the accident. We'll take one helicopter, our paramedics another. Luci, spread the word for anyone with diving experience or gear. When you find them, get them there.''

Armando turned, snapping orders, assigning chores, picking teams. He put Laura on the team staying at the hospital.

As the team he'd picked for the field prepared themselves, she stood, fists on hips, glaring at him.

"Watch out, Armando!" Arsenio chuckled. "You'd better duck if you want to live to see your child born!''

Armando stiffened, an involuntary glance jerking to Laura, to her belly. His child.

His child!

Everyone had taken the news of Laura's pregnancy in their stride, assuming what he'd wanted them to assume: that the child was his and that was why she'd broken up with Diego.

Arsenio had been grilling him about it ever since, calling him the son of a gun who'd had Laura dropping Diego as if he'd never been. He'd gone on to say it made sense. *They* fit together. Then had come the endless questions. Had they played it cool, kept their hands off each other for Diego's sake? But what had kept them at odds after he'd died? Tough times coming to terms with their relationship?

Arsenio, his best friend. He really disliked him now.

"Yes, *do* duck, Armando," Laura snarled. "I thought we're done with the helpless pregnant women baloney!''

"Not helpless, but even you have to admit that being pregnant does make a difference. More every day." He turned to leave, not giving her time to argue. "There'll be plenty of hard work here.''

She ran after him. "I want to be with *you*.''

Don't make me love you any more, he almost shouted, pain

shooting past his chest to his throat, his eyes. He blinked, shook his head, not looking at her.

"Last time you split us up…" She squeezed his arm, fingers digging in, right down to his soul. *I almost lost you,* he completed in his mind. No persuasion could have hit harder.

He still couldn't look at her, and turned to the others. "OK. Myra, you're staying in Laura's place, Arsenio, you in Jason's. Let's go, people."

Minutes later, they were in the air. Laura curved into him as they discussed their intervention based on the reports starting to come in from their paramedics who'd arrived at the site.

Armando did what he'd become an expert in—functioning on two levels. His superficial focus on work, his profound one on Laura.

She wanted to be with him.

It should have reassured him, soothed his torment. It didn't.

Why should he fear losing her, when he didn't really have her? When it seemed he never would?

"What do you think you're doing?"

At her shout, Armando threw her a preoccupied glance over his shoulder as he kicked off his shoes, then stripped down to his pants. Laura jumped from the helicopter and raced to him, hung on his arm.

"Relax. This strip show isn't for you."

She grimaced at his untimely humor. "The two unaccounted-for children are either on their way to La Clínica, long drowned or swept away by the current. Anyway, others are searching, *with* diving gear!"

He disentangled himself calmly, patted her gently. "I'm not crazy enough to brave the river depths unequipped. One of the rescue men blacked out and was dragged out. They're getting me his gear. There are only three men down there and they need all the help they can get. I am the only one left up here with diving experience."

The diving gear was delivered in seconds, and he stood

there accepting the rescue workers' help in getting kitted up for his underwater search. As soon as they finished and without another word or look, he waded into the water, dived in and disappeared.

The moment the water engulfed him Laura's mind erupted with dread.

"Armando!"

She barely heard Jason's reprimand. "See why you shouldn't be on the same team, Laura?"

"It's freezing—and the current... Oh, God, Jason..."

"He's a big boy, Laura. He knows what he's doing." Jason jerked his head towards the two dozen people who needed help. "C'mon, let him do what he can and let's do our part."

Her logic said he was right. But her heart was crumpling, knowing Armando and how far he'd go for others. Jason prodded her away from the river bank and she stumbled over to where the others were disembarking from the helicopter, hauling bags and blankets with the paramedics' help.

"Our paras say resuscitation was superb, even before they arrived," Susan said. "The widespread CPR and basic resuscitation courses La Clínica and GAO sponsored in the province has really paid off. Dozens were saved thanks to bystanders' efforts."

"But others weren't." Constanza came back, running. "More still doubtful. OK, non-Spanish speakers, brought you a status report. Forty-nine people already dispatched, half of them at La Clínica by now, between ambulatory and distressed. The twenty-three remaining here were rescued much later, some just as we arrived, so we're looking at worse conditions and prognoses. Initial assessment and resuscitation applied, triage says eight range from unresponsive to distressed. No one's been pronounced dead yet, though, so let's see what we can do to keep it that way. Laura?"

Laura heard, barely understood. *Focus,* she berated herself. *Armando can take care of himself. Lead your team in his stead. See to your patients.*

She took a deep breath, forcing her professional self into the driver's seat. "OK, here's the plan. Most serious cases to helicopters and ambulances now! Watch out for associated injuries beside the hypoxia and acidosis of near-drowning. Those people are all high-risk for spinal and head injuries—hell, *every* sort of injury with that fall off the bridge. We'll split the serious ones. Anyone needs help, yell. Right—*go*!"

As everyone rushed to their patients, it was she who couldn't move. Armando had been down there for only minutes, but it felt like for ever. What if he blacked out, too? What if something went wrong? What if he got trapped inside one of the submerged vehicles and his oxygen ran out? No matter what she told herself, nothing else mattered.

Susan took her arm and she dragged her away. "He'll be all right!"

Laura moved, but the ticking inside her that had started with Armando's disappearance underwater went on, each tick counting down her moments of control. She still managed to concentrate on the victim she'd picked, a three-year-old unresponsive boy.

After thirty minutes of futile resuscitation efforts, and since he wasn't even hypothermic, she had to pronounce him dead. Then Constanza pulled her out of the helicopter, and out of range of the wailing mother.

"You did all you could. We all did. Let's go see what that stubborn husband of yours is doing."

Laura was shattered. Armando's danger was the only thing mitigating the trauma of losing a casualty, and a child too. If that was what losing a child she didn't know felt like, what would it be like to lose her own? What would the boy's mother do? How could she live on?

"'Super Armando'—that's what we used to call him!"

What...? Constanza had been talking all the time. That eventually penetrated Laura's distraught fog. "You, too? When?"

"When we were growing up together. Didn't Diego mention it?"

Constanza grew up with Armando? That was news to her. But, then, what did she really know about him? No more than what he knew about her, which amounted to almost no hard facts. During the month they'd been husband and wife for real, they had rarely had time for a proper conversation, all their discussions revolving around work—or passion. Every moment they snatched for themselves was spent making love.

"We were all first, second and third cousins, and Armando was the oldest. *Dios*, how we looked up to him then." Constanza chuckled, the look in her eyes as she looked down at Laura envious. She still wanted him.

Her and the rest of the female species!

But this woman is beautiful, Laura thought. It never ceased to amaze her just how beautiful. Yet Armando wouldn't look at her, or at any other woman. He'd given his word, his pledge—as long as they remained married. That meant for ever...

They'd reached the river bank again and stood watching the ongoing rescue and salvage efforts under the rapidly encroaching night.

Armando—oh, please, please, my love. Stop. Come out. I need you!

Suddenly shouts resounded as a diver broke the water surface with a limp child in his arms. *Armando!*

Laura felt her feet running, heard his name reiterated on sobs as she waded into the water. People crowded her, making her stumble back under their combined eagerness. Constanza was still beside her, still talking.

"'Super Armando' saves the day again. He saved Diego from drowning once, you know? Not to mention from a dozen other predicaments." Constanza paused, sighed. "Poor, foolish Diego." That turned Laura's eyes to her against her will. "He really should have picked a lesser man to emulate, to rival. He should have resisted the urge to show you off to him.

He should have known you'd drop him the second you laid eyes on Armando!''

Laura heard Armando's growling baritone ordering people away as he strode to their helicopter. Then she heard nothing more as Constanza's words echoed in her mind, filling it, knocking down defenses and self-delusions.

Was that what she'd done? Dropped Diego because of Armando?

As they reached the helicopter, and Armando handed the limp girl to Jason and Susan, his exhausted eyes searched for her, found her. And she faced it then.

She had. She'd slashed Diego to pieces, seen everything wrong with him, punished him for not being her ideal—for not being Armando!

As he'd led me to believe he was, she tried to defend herself to that voice of truth inside her. *And I didn't know then that Armando was my ideal...*

Oh, yes, you knew, the voice lashed her. *You took one look at him and were crazy for him. You went out to rid yourself of Diego any way you could. Your right, of course, but Diego loved you in his own way, imperfections and misconceptions and all. You could have left him, yet given him some dignity. You didn't have to drive him mad, drive him to his death...*

"Laura—are you all right?" Armando's anxious question fractured guilt's crushing grasp. She re-entered reality with a sickening thud.

She rushed to him, helped him off with his diving gear, helped him on with his clothes, then covered him with a blanket a paramedic passed her.

"Am *I* all right?" She wanted to hit him. Push him to the ground and kiss every inch of him. Burst into tears. "You're the one who's been down there in the freezing water almost an hour! What were you hoping for after all that time? I just lost a boy who'd been submerged for only minutes!"

"The freezing water is what's keeping me hopeful we may yet resuscitate this little girl!"

Laura didn't answer as they boarded the helicopter and

Armando directed Romero to fly them to La Clínica at once. Her mind raced, remembering long-unused medical information.

She was aware that severe hypothermia, while usually a cause of death, could actually be a life-saver in long submerging. The water temperature with the brutal cold front that Argentina's winter brought must be way below 70°F, making this cold, almost freezing-water drowning. It was within the realm of possibility that even a seemingly dead victim could be resuscitated by extended CPR and returning body temperature to normal. Hopefully without significant central nervous system damage.

As they took off, Armando asked, "Your casualty wasn't hypothermic, was he?"

"No," she said dully. "He also had a head injury. All signs of a massive subdural hematoma."

"Barring other serious injuries, and hoping her diving reflex worked, sustained resuscitation may yet save her. And even if not, I couldn't overlook that possibility."

Laura knew that the "diving reflex" was a mammalian reflex triggered by the face hitting cold water. It reduced blood supply to skin and muscles, saving it for the heart and brain. The younger the individual, the stronger the reflex. It was the first defense mechanism against drowning in cold water. From then on, as the body's core temperature plunged, severe hypothermia slowed down metabolism and oxygen consumption to almost nil, so that vital organs survived even long oxygen deprivation.

But as far as she could remember, the reflex stopped working the moment the victim was fished out of the water, starting cellular death. Immediate and aggressive resuscitation was needed if there was to be any hope of saving the little girl.

Jason had already cut off the girl's wet, cold clothes and had her wrapped in warm, dry blankets. She heard Armando asking him, his voice wavering with his violent shivering, "Is she pulseless?"

"Yes, not one beat over 45 seconds," Jason said.

"Rectal temperature is 60° Fahrenheit, Armando," Constanza said.

Laura added a blanket around Armando and poured him a hot cup of coffee to correct his own hypothermia. He gulped it down as he directed them in the resuscitation procedure.

"Start CPR. Susan, mouth to mask, 120 chest compressions. Constanza, get me a twelve-lead electrocardiogram. If it's ventricular fibrillation, deliver up to three shocks, followed by bretylium-lidocaine bolus. If confirmed asystole in two leads, you know the protocol of medications. Jason, start aggressive rewarming. Let's use everything, external and internal. Warm packs to head, neck, abdomen, armpits and groin. And warmed IV saline—make it 108°F."

"How about warmed oxygen?" Jason asked.

"We'd need to intubate then, and this is going to be one difficult intubation, with her so spastic. Dangerous, too, since it could cause VF if we manage to get a heartbeat."

"Leave it to me. As the resident anesthesiologist, I'm the best qualified to handle it." Jason said, already preparing for the intubation.

By that time Laura had made a complete check of the girl. "No other apparent associated injuries. No reflexes, pupils unresponsive, widely dilated. There must be severe cerebral swelling."

Armando met her eyes. "Lasix and phenobarbitone now!" he said, then tried to join in the resusciation efforts.

"No." Laura made him sit back. "You rest until we get back. I have a feeling this little girl is going to need your skills in the OR."

They arrived at La Clínica in thirty minutes and, as Laura had predicted, the still pulseless girl had to be rushed to the OR. They continued CPR, keeping her circulation and breathing going as they prepared her for cardiopulmonary bypass via femoral artery access. This was the best way to warm her blood and bring her core temperature back to normal.

After three hours, they disconnected her from the bypass

machine and took her to Intensive Care, finally with a spontaneous pulse and respiration.

She wasn't out of the woods yet—there were so many complications that could still occur—but she *was* alive. Thanks to Armando. That girl owed her life to his tenacity, his knowledge.

As they walked out of Intensive care, Laura rubbed his back lovingly, hooked her arm in his, breathed against his chest, "Super Armando!"

He glanced down at her in surprise. Then he laughed. "Who told you my secret identity?" He quirked an eyebrow, not looking "super" at all at that moment but gaunt and spent.

"Your number one fan, of course!"

His other eyebrow rose in incredulity. "And who's that?"

She opened her mouth to say "Constanza", to tease him about his effect on women. She didn't. This was an opportunity she had to take. To assuage her guilt, to make amends, to spread better memories of Diego, the man who'd fathered her child. The man she'd gravely wronged. Starting with reinforcing Armando's love for him. She breathed the lie, the soft longing to rewrite history. "Diego, of course. Who else?"

Time passed. Nothing changed.

Or it did. For the worse. And worse.

For the first time in his life, Armando started to empathize with people who broke down, lost their minds.

Laura. It all came down to Laura. He sent her crazy with passion, challenged and satisfied her mind, shared her humor, commanded her total personal and professional respect. Night after night he made her his, deeper, fuller. And day after day he told himself it was more than enough, more than most men even dreamed of having.

It wasn't enough. He needed to permeate her heart, enslave her soul, own them, like she did his. He needed all that to function, to maintain his mental health—maybe even to survive. And apart from the laughter, the camaraderie, the unbridled passion, what did he have? What did she give him? Memories of Diego!

Didn't she realize what she was doing to him, always bringing Diego up with such longing regret? How could he have been so wrong about the depth of her emotional involvement with Diego? He'd believed their relationship had been superficial and quickly aborted. But had it been more? And *that* much more? On her side at least?

Violent, ugly emotions preyed on him, subjugating him, damaging him. He would have welcomed the emotional dependence if it hadn't been coupled with corrosive jealousy. And guilt. How could he harbor such venom for Diego now he was dead?

But being dead didn't turn him into a saint! And that was how Laura was painting him. He didn't begrudge her her memories, but they seemed to be denying him access to her heart…

"MVA victims being flown in in a few minutes, Armando."

He turned to her, the focus of all his hopes and despair. At seven months pregnant she was glorious, radiating health and sensuality. She burned ever brighter at his touch, insatiable, divine. Just minutes ago, he'd taken her, twice, almost without a breath in between, back there in his office, getting creative to make allowance for her changing shape. As he'd possessed her she'd moaned her eagerness for the next time, the next variation on their loving. He'd thought he'd die with too much love, too hard a pleasure…

Work. Snap out of it. He cleared his throat, asked, "Any reports from the paramedics on the way?"

"A head-on car crash, the only victims a man and a woman. The man was driving without a seat belt. He's critical. The woman isn't—so far."

His heart kicked at the subdued note in her voice. "Sounds too much like your accident."

She didn't comment. No time to. At least, he wanted to

believe that. The paramedics had burst in with their casualties, shouting that the man had arrested.

In seconds they'd implemented the practiced protocols of defibrillation.

After almost fifteen minutes of failed attempts to get a sustainable heart rhythm, they had to declare the man dead. The woman was rushed to the OR for an emergency laparotomy.

As he and Laura scrubbed side by side, it all replayed in his mind. The hours when he'd failed to put Diego back together, when he'd almost lost her. Lost her…

A tremulous sigh escaped her. "That poor guy, so young, dead so needlessly…"

"Don't you mean that poor woman? She had nothing to do with what happened to her. The man on the other hand—when you drive recklessly, you really have it coming. It's just criminal to take others with you on your way out!"

She turned on him, her color high. "It isn't always so black and white. Take Diego, for instance. He'd come after me, and after we had this row he just lost control. Surely someone who'd been driving sensibly all his life didn't deserve to die if they lost control once!"

Diego. Again. No. No more.

"No, he wouldn't, but we're not talking about someone like that. We're talking about a man who drank and drove. And if you want to talk about Diego, it was a marvel he didn't die before he did, the way he went through life, daring fate, not caring whom he hurt while he got his thrills. That wasn't his first reckless driving accident, but it was his last! Why don't you open your eyes, Laura? St. Diego was an irresponsible wretch who killed his parents before their time with worry and grief. He almost killed you. And, you know, what's more, he wasn't only wild, he was manipulative and cruel. From day one he saw how I wanted you. He delighted in taunting me about you, in throwing us closer, to show me he had the woman I wanted, to twist the knife and watch me squirm!"

CHAPTER TEN

"WHOA!"

"Don't give me 'whoa', give me direct pressure, quick!"

Armando watched Laura glancing at Jason above her mask, that weird brightness to her tone and eyes.

"Myra, non-crushing vascular clamp." Myra was already handing her the clamp she needed, and he watched her deft hands cross-clamping the abdominal aorta, gaining hemorrhage control in seconds.

"That was some fountain." Jason whistled. "Good thing we're stocked up on blood and blood constituents. That flood really got people responding to La Clínica's and GAO's joint donation campaign."

Laura nodded. "That's a silver lining for you. Suction, please." She waited until Myra irrigated the abdominal cavity and cleared the operative field of the obscuring blood, then turned to him. "OK, Armando, that's the liver sewn up and the aorta clamped. Going for direct suturing, or grafting to repair the artery?"

"Myra?" He looked at his nurse.

Myra shook her head. "She's not hemodynamically stable enough for prolonged procedures. BP fell to 80 over 40 and isn't improving much with either transfusion or cross-clamping."

He looked back at Laura. "There you have it. Grafting is out." He ordered the necessary suture material and instruments, and in seconds, with both Laura and Jason keeping the abdominal organs out of the way and the whole length of the abdominal aorta exposed, he repaired the artery.

"Are you going for splenorrhaphy?"

He stared at Laura for a second too long, got the expected raised brows. He didn't know what to make of her attitude.

He *shouldn't* make anything of it. Not now anyway. "Repair the spleen if you like. Or leave it till the end. As you can see, it isn't a significant source of bleeding. I think now that we've taken care of the aorta we have something far more insidious to worry about. I suspect retroperitoneal bleeding."

"Ah, at last something different from my own injuries. I was thinking it was a case of *déjà vu*."

"It isn't," he almost snapped, her strange lightness jarring him. "Her injuries are far more serious. Her intraperitoneal hemorrhage was the immediate threat, and I know we didn't even have time for an X-ray, but I suspect a complex pelvic lateral compression injury with iliac bone fracture. I think ongoing pelvic arterial bleeding is causing her instability now."

"If you say so." Was that a *grin* behind her mask?

"And, if so, are you packing the bleeding or are you going for definitive measures?" Jason asked.

He transferred his attention to Jason before he roared *What's to grin about?* at Laura. "Now we have angiographic facilities in the OR, thanks to GAO and you guys, I say we find out the exact location of the bleeding then embolize it."

In minutes, they'd injected their patient with the contrast material that would enter her bloodstream and opacify arteries that were usually translucent in X-rays. Soon they were looking at the woman's pelvis in the angio machine, the radio-opaque material seeping out where the artery was cut, pinpointing the exact site of injury. There was free hemorrhage from the pudendal artery and complete cut-off of the anterior division of the internal iliac artery in her pelvis.

"Gelfoam, Myra," Armando demanded.

The efficient woman already had the necessary injection ready, and he performed the embolization, injecting the clot of Gelfoam under X-ray guidance right into the injured artery blocking it and stopping the bleeding, then coiling and blocking the severed artery.

"Whoa, again," Jason said. "That's what I call rapid stabilization."

"Uncanny diagnosis as usual, Armando," Laura said, her tone impressed. So why did it oppress him to be on the receiving end of her professional adulation this time?

He dismissed the praise. "When you've been at it as long as I have, you tend to develop an extra sense about it all."

"In that case, I'd like to introduce you to some of my sixty-year-old professors who never developed any sense at all!" Jason guffawed.

Laura laughed too, but didn't comment, didn't return his searching glance. She just went ahead and repaired the spleen, checked the abdomen for further injuries one last time, then left it to Jason, who'd been keen to expand his surgical experience, to close up and place drains, chattering and joking all the time. Soon their patient was neatly closed up and transferred to Critical Care for further monitoring.

He followed Laura out of the OR. "Great job, as usual." He removed her cap from her head, smoothed his hand over the burnished blackness he worshiped. Usually, she'd press her head into his grasp, tilt an eager face up, mouth gasping for his, his tongue, his passion. She didn't this time. She kept on walking, taking the rest of her surgical gear off.

"You too—as usual. You really amaze me sometimes." Her tone was still light. It didn't fool his heart.

After that stunned look with which she'd received his tirade, she hadn't given any outward indication of her real reaction. She'd become opaque. Worse—different! The others clearly thought her lightness normal. He *knew* it wasn't. And it was far worse than if she'd been indignant or angry. What was she thinking? *Dios*, when and how would his punishment come?

"Laura…"

She spoke at the same time, didn't offer to hear him out first. "I'll make my rounds, a couple of calls then I'm going back…to the house to put my feet up."

Hesitation, then "to the house". Not home. His heart convulsed once, then again—harder. That subtle change in her breathing, her color, the tension in her face. Was this just a physical manifestation of whatever emotions she was suppressing, or was it more?

Guilt kicked inside him. Whatever it was, *he* was behind all her physical and emotional stress, making love to her, blowing up in her face. "You've done enough today. I'm taking you home."

A quick step ahead extricated her from his anxious grasp. "No, you're not. You still have that meeting with Howard and I still have to phone Burnside Foundation to hurry those maternity and contraceptive care leaflets."

He paused. His meeting with Zimmerman was important. He'd been out of the country recruiting staff for La Clínica's GAO-sponsored intensive care unit, taking over Diego's old job. He was bringing all the candidates' résumés for him to pick from. Not that Armando cared about any of that now. Laura was shutting him out, looking—feeling—fragile. Nothing else mattered, existed.

But she was already walking away.

Run after her, tell her you're sorry, that you didn't mean it, that it's too complicated, not as black and white as you made it sound. Tell her you were just fed up, insecure…

He remained rooted to the spot until she disappeared from his view. Then his cellphone rang and it was Zimmerman. *Later.* He made the shaky promise to himself.

He'd fix everything later. Once and for all.

"Laura—I'm home, *querida*!"

Silence. Still so weird. For the months the flood refugees had stayed with them it had been bedlam. Then they had gone, and the switch to silence had almost been a shock. Laura had joked that they'd become so conditioned to making love with a crowd just outside their door, whether at home or at work, it must have perverted their sexual tendencies. That they'd find the solitude a turn-off. It hadn't, of course. The freedom to move around the house naked, to make love anywhere, had only intensified the already raging inferno between them.

Today the silence was ominous, carrying Laura's withdrawal.

A thought hit him, almost buckling his legs. He doubled back, ran outside and around the house. Her car!

It was there by the kitchen entrance. He almost fell to his knees in relief. For a moment, he'd almost convinced himself she'd left...

And why should he think that? Insecure was too mild a word to describe him. They'd just had a row. Not even that. He'd said a few things he shouldn't have and she must be ticked off, but that was all. He'd apologize, explain, then take her in his arms. Love her, cherish her. Everything would be fine.

As he walked back into the house the eerie silence hit him again. His nerves went haywire once more. What if she was sick? Fear propelled him up the stairs. In seconds he was bursting into the master bedroom, *their* bedroom now.

Laura was there, not sick, just looking out the window at the arid acres extending as far as the eye could see. She didn't even turn at his violent entry.

Pain slammed inside him. Her approval, her attention were crucial to his existence. He couldn't have her love, but he'd had those at least, in abundance. Now suddenly they were no more. And it gutted him, weakened him.

His anxious stride took him to her, took her to him, filling his arms, her back to his front. He buried his longing in her neck, his mouth opening on the proof of her life, his hands gliding on the proof of life growing within her. "I'm sorry, *mi amor*. So sorry. For what I said last night. Forgive me, please."

No answer. Not even a breath. And she was so cold. He'd worry about her inner coldness later. The central heating hadn't been fixed and this August had brought the most bitter cold Argentina had seen in years. It had been a fateful year all around.

"*Querida*, let me warm you." He didn't wait for assent, just swept her to their bed, silencing any protest in voracious kisses, stripping her and himself and fusing their bodies under the slowly warming electric blanket.

Usually, she would have been frantic to get closer, to kiss deeper, to merge faster. This time, as her body responded, emerald irises shrinking as her pupils dilated, breathing catching, heat surging in her limbs, there was no volition to it all. She didn't want it!

No! It was all he had of her. He'd make her want it. Want him.

He freed her hair from its braided prison, buried his hands and face in its beloved luxuriance, spilled all his longing in her ears, in Spanish, counting on how it always inflamed her.

Her arousal mounted. He felt it, smelled it, yet her hands went to his, pushing them away. "Stop, Armando…"

No, no! He couldn't stop. She didn't want him to stop. She was just punishing him, not even bent on it, ordering him to stop in that hot, hungry moan.

He claimed her breasts, dragging out her cries of pleasure. His fingers sought her depths, teased, fondled, filled, and in only seconds received her body's homage.

"*Si, amor, si*, take it all, give it to me," he encouraged her, starving for her pleasure, drawing it out. Then more, until she was writhing again.

This time she dragged his head to hers, turned on her side, presenting him with her back in the position they now made love in.

She still wanted him! Nothing had changed, or would ever change.

"*Mi amor…*" He stroked into her, with all the gentleness and care of his love and longing. "*Te amo Laura—te amo, te amo…*" His confessions accentuated each silken glide, each slash of pleasure in his body, each cry of abandon calling out to him, right until the moment release buffeted them.

Subsiding inside her had never brought that much peace. After anxiety had almost wrecked him, the security of having her again—knowing his love, and whatever it was she felt for him, would conquer anything—made him serene, invincible.

She moved. He hardened again, grimaced at his helpless reaction, withdrew. Later, when the baby was born, he promised himself. He'd let go then, really show her how he wanted her. He was sure she'd welcome and match anything he had in mind. For now he had to keep it to this level. He wanted her and the baby safe, more than he wanted to live.

"Armando…"

Sunset threw weak gold over her open face and gilded skin. Satiation still quivered on her lips, filled her eyes, her voice. He added the sight to the tendernesses filling him for her, smoothing her in sweeping motions, reveling in the freedom, the privilege. *"Si, mi corazón?"*

"I want a divorce."

Laura was back at the window, dressed once more, this time staring into the darkness, the only proof of time's passage. In the void she'd hurled him into, there was nothing—no sense, no sensation, not even pain. Not yet.

Armando must have still been functioning on some level, for he heard her ragged words when she finally spoke. "I'll…move out right now and—and I hope you'll conclude the—the official steps of the…divorce as soon as you can…"

The *divorce*. She'd said it again. This was real. She meant it! *No!*

He was on his feet, surging towards her, the need to stop her mutilating words bursting his heart. She turned sharply, warding him off, almost lost her balance. He reached for her, only for her trembling *Don't touch me* to freeze him, inside and out. Arms that were no longer his to move, to feel, dropped to his side.

"Please—just… Please! You—you said—you *promised* it would end if it wasn't working…"

The enormity of the falsehood dissolved his paralysis. "Not working? Nothing ever worked better. We just finished proving how much it's working…"

"That was just sex!"

He took the blow head on, ground his teeth, went on. "*Just* the most damn phenomenal sex. And everything else is working, as spectacularly."

Rejection hardened on her face. His confusion, his heartache shuddered out of him on a despairing groan. "*Por Dios*, Laura—why?"

"You lied to me!" The ragged, quiet accusation was a death sentence. "You made me think you loved Diego. But you despise him—hate him even. You're still jealous of him even now he's long dead."

"No, no, Laura. You misunderstood me…"

"I did, for long months. I no longer do. I understood you very well for the first time last night."

"*Querida*, no—just listen…"

"No, you listen, Armando. I thought you'd be the best father I could give my daughter. Now I know better. The way you hate her father, any man would be a better father to her than you."

"That's not true. I didn't hate him, and I will love her—I *do* love her as my own—"

She cut him off. "Can you look me in the eye and tell me you don't hate it that she isn't yours for real?"

He couldn't. Every time someone referred to the baby as his child, a red-hot spear twisted in his heart. But it wasn't with hatred or jealousy. It was with—with… If only he could put his feelings into words…

He tried, sounded lame, ridiculous. "It's not the way you think, the way you're implying!"

"I don't care what way it is. You hate her father, you hate her not being yours, and you will hate *her*. Well, she's the only reason I married you and the best thing I can do for her is leave you.''

No! She was turning away. She was really leaving him. He couldn't let her go. Couldn't survive without her. He had to hang onto her, no matter what it took.

But how could he do that? Even after all they'd been through, all he thought he'd become to her, she still didn't love him. Didn't even care. And now she no longer trusted or believed in him, her only reason for marrying him was gone with her trust and belief.

He had to think fast. Laura was exiling him from their lives, considering him an outsider, a threat even. But she and her baby would always be the only family he had. The only family he wanted. The family he'd go to any lengths just to be near. He had to be in their lives, in any capacity, on any terms.

Even if it meant giving them up.

Laura dragged her two suitcases out, blind, suffocating.

She could no longer bear looking at him. She had to get out of there fast. She'd succumbed twice already tonight. She'd succumb for ever if she didn't use the momentum of her realization.

But, oh, lord, what was going on in his mind behind the fierce expression? *Was* it possible for him to love Diego's child if he hated Diego? Resented him at least, was jealous of him? And did his jealousy mean he loved *her*?

And if he did, why wasn't he coming after her, again and again? Overriding her accusations, demolishing her fears? He'd objected to her words, said she'd misunderstood, that it wasn't how she thought. So why wasn't he saying exactly how it was? Telling her he loved her, proving to her he didn't hate her baby for not being his?

And how will he prove that? that brutally honest voice sneered. *You're just like the mother you hated all your life! The mother who chose her lover, her addiction to his pleasures, her subjugation to his every wish, over her own daugh-*

ter. The daughter of the boring husband she was glad to be rid of…

No! No, she wasn't. And Armando wasn't like her stepfather!

How can you know? Jealousy and hatred turn men to demons. Everyone thought your stepfather was a good man, and look what he did to you!

She felt Armando moving slowly towards her, coming to stand behind her. She couldn't bear it any more and turned. She found him staring down at her, his expression unfathomable, the largest piece of her soul.

Oh, Armando, please—help me. Say you love me like I love you, say you'll overcome your demons for my love…

Hesitant hands reached for hers, carried them to his mouth. He kissed them, breathed hot, ragged longing into her flesh. She knew then. She couldn't leave him. She'd do anything to make both him and her baby happy…

Then he pressed her hands to his heart. "If you insist," he started, his voice bottomless, his words slow, "I'll give you a divorce, Laura. You can still register me as your baby's father, but I won't come near her, if that's what you want. But that doesn't have to be the end—it can be an even better beginning. If you think the marriage isn't working, I have a proposition for you—for what we both know works between us. Sex—no strings, unbridled and when it suits you. And work. Wait till you hear the plans I have for La Clínica, plans only you can help me realize."

She stared at him, her hopes, her world ending.

An endless moment later she let all her horror and anger and anguish out before they crushed her. "A better beginning? I'll tell you what's the *best* beginning for me. To never see you or this country ever again."

CHAPTER ELEVEN

"YOU are crazy, aren't you?"

Laura carefully turned to Constanza. "And I always had the highest esteem of your mental faculties too, Constanza."

The taller woman glared down at her. "Spare me the smart-alec routine, Laura. There may not be any love lost between us but…"

"There isn't?" It was a genuine question. She really liked Constanza and, apart from the understandable envy, had never picked up any antipathy from her. Or maybe she'd been too filled with Armando to really register anything else.

"OK, so you're the one who has him and can afford to be above such pettiness. What's really driving me crazy is that you're throwing him away!"

"Shouldn't you be glad I am? So you'll get your chance with him?" Her lips said it, but her mind couldn't even contemplate it. Constanza or any other woman with Armando! The horror, the loss was too great to grasp. She'd have the rest of her life to get her mind around the enormity of it.

And it was her own doing.

"Oh, believe me, if he ever gives me one longer-than-usual look, I'll be all over him. Not that he ever has or probably ever will. Not after what you've done to him. How can you leave him this way? And after all he's done for you!"

"My time with GAO in Argentina is over—"

"*Dios*, but you're cold! First you kill Diego and don't even shed a tear over him, now you're killing Armando, walking out with his unborn daughter!"

"It isn't the way you think, the way you're implying…" Armando's words. She hadn't listened to him when he'd said them less than a week ago. Constanza wasn't listening to her now.

"I don't care what way it is. My cousin, a great man, is suffering, being destroyed, and he's all I care about. But maybe once you're gone he'll be cured, he'll be the Armando we know and love again. I intended to try to talk you out of leaving, but not now. Go away, Laura. And good riddance!"

The glorious woman turned on her heel and stormed out of Laura's consultation room, leaving her shaking, the ever-ready tears spilling again.

This was her last day in Argentina. GAO had been stunned by, then resistant to her request for relocation. In the end they'd succumbed, but had insisted she stay at La Clínica to her last day to finalize her business and arrange for her replacement. And here she was, breathing the same air as Armando, dying with every breath, then forced to live again. Only for her baby.

Nothing could make it worse. Not that even her own team thought she was the scum of the earth, breaking up a family and crippling a devoted husband. Nothing could hurt any more. Not after listening to Armando giving her up so easily, without even a token fight. He'd said once he'd like the marriage to work, but that if it didn't, then it didn't. It was that simple. After all they'd had, all she'd thought they'd had, her only relevance in his life remained the same. Sex. And work.

His intensity, his jealousy hadn't been love. Or even possessiveness. Just macho pride. It made no difference to him if she was his wife or occasional sex partner. He'd agreed to the divorce as if it was a relief, a liberation, offered the no-strings affair as if he'd been wishing for it all along. Just like being released from taking part in her baby's life. And, like Diego, he thought she had the money and the means to help him realize his grand projects.

Her harsh refusal to his proposition had been a desperate plea for him to hang onto her, a last-ditch attempt to scare him into realizing he cared more than he'd thought. But as his eyes emptied she'd been the one who'd lost her mind with fear. She'd prayed for him to, please, *please*, dismiss her refusal, give her a chance to take back her rejection and the crumbs he'd offered.

But she hadn't even been worth that effort to him. Sex he'd get somewhere else, and work would go on without her.

He'd just turned, dressed and walked out of the room. He'd even loaded her bags in her car. Hadn't even stood around until she'd driven away. Then for the next week, as she'd prepared to leave Argentina, he hadn't said another word to her. That was how much he cared.

"Let it go, Armando!" Arsenio called out, slowing his friend's steps towards his four-by-four. "There's nothing you can do about it."

"We'll see." He threw the extra emergency bag in the back, jumped in. Arsenio was at his window, agitated, angry.

"Let the police handle this."

"It's the police that's causing the crisis—and the injuries. And I have to get Lucianna's son and husband out of there. Luigi's injured and from the sounds of it he won't last until the siege is lifted. Even if Lucianna wasn't like a mother to me and Luigi like a brother, I wouldn't leave anyone to bleed to death if I could help it."

"But how will you get through the siege?"

"I know all the ins and outs of the factory, all the ways in the police won't be covering."

"But why sneak in? Why not just go to the police forces, tell them who you are and that you have a casualty inside you must get to?"

"You think they'd let me patch up the people inside so they'd be able to hold out longer? I don't think so."

"But there've been reports of exchanges of fire. What if you get caught in the crossfire? Just what are trying to do— kill yourself?"

Armando revved the motor. "Step away, Arsenio."

"Don't be stupid, *amigo*. At least let me come with you."

"You're my second in command, Arsenio. You stay here and take care of La Clínica. Now, move."

Arsenio stepped back, raising both hands in disgust. Armando roared away.

The call for help had come just in time. He had to be somewhere away from La Clínica, the worse the crisis the better. Something to save his sanity, to stop him counting down Laura's remaining hours in Argentina.

But Arsenio couldn't be more wrong about him trying to kill himself. He'd cling to life for as long as she breathed. Even if she was for ever lost to him.

"Slow down, Lucianna." Laura held the weeping woman by the shoulders, tried to steady her. And herself. She couldn't have understood correctly. It must be her still dodgy Spanish and Lucianna's sobbing. But she was sure she got two things right. Armando, over and over—and injured.

She turned frantic eyes to anyone who'd explain. Both Arsenio and Constanza were heading their way.

"What is it?" she cried.

"What do you care?" Constanza spat. "Isn't your time here up? This is about local trouble and Armando. Neither concern you anymore."

"Constanza, enough! See to Lucianna."

Constanza gave her another scathing glare as she obeyed Arsenio. Laura wouldn't have felt anything if she'd slapped her. She clung to Arsenio's arm. "Please!"

He heaved in a huge sigh. "You've heard about the factories that were abandoned by their owners after the collapse, leaving workers without pay or work? Well, a lot of those were commandeered by those workers, who got production up and running again, with better output and real worker satisfaction. Some owners came back with court orders to enforce their ownership, not only taking over all the workers' achievements but denying them any rights in the new order they'd created. Last night, the owners of Lucianna's husband's and son's factory brought a police force to evict the workers. They refused to go and things got out of control. They're besieged inside now.''

''And Armando's there? Injured?''

''There's been a call, not really clear, but…''

She was no longer listening, already running, ignoring Arsenio's exclamation, escaping his detaining grasp. She got her emergency kit, grabbed one of the nurses, made him give her a ride to the factory, to Armando.

Armando.

If she'd had doubts before, they were no more. She didn't care what happened to her, and subsequently to her daughter.

Only he mattered.

Laura watched in horror as a policeman got close enough to one of the factory's ground-floor windows. Seconds later, his tear-gas grenade exploded inside the factory. A few seconds more brought a handful of men staggering out. But not Armando. Where was he? Was he too injured to walk out? God—no, *no*!

Another round of fire came from the third floor, along with incensed roars. The police retaliated, hitting more windows, doing the factory more damage.

The thunder of approaching vehicles distracted Laura from the unfolding nightmare. Her blood froze as she watched armored soldiers with heavy weaponry jumping down from army vehicles.

Oh, God. They were ending the crisis and making an example of those workers, no matter what level of force they had to use. She couldn't let that happen.

She sprang from her hiding place. ''Stop, you fools. Stop!''

At her screaming approach everyone turned towards her, cocking their weapons. One fired a shot. It whizzed by her head. It didn't even slow her down.

The squad's commander barked orders for them to take position in case she was a diversion. Two covered her as she ran up to him, feeling her for any hidden weapons in the thickness of her thermal clothing.

"What do you think you're going to do?" she screamed in the commander's face. "Kill those men inside for refusing to give up their work, their factory, to those who'd abandoned them and it, who're coming in now to take everything and throw them out on the streets?"

"Why are you speaking English? Who are you?" the soldier growled. "And—*Madre de Dios*—you're pregnant!"

"So what if I am? I'm also an American and a doctor—head of GAO mission in Argentina. And my husband, La Clínica's director, is in there!"

"What's he doing in there?"

"Helping people you injured—what else? Now, hold your fire and let me go inside. You've managed to injure *him* too, you monsters!"

The man took her angry blow in his chest with great control. "We're just doing our jobs. And we can't let you inside. They're pretty jumpy and might fire at you, too. What if you get killed? We have enough local trouble, we don't need an international incident on our hands."

"Don't you have a megaphone? I'll talk to them, they'll let me in."

In seconds they'd brought her a megaphone. She held it to her lips and suddenly only tears came. Armando—he might not be able to hear her any more.

No! He had to be alive, she had to save him. He had to hear her!

"Armando, it's Laura…" Tears spilled, words choked. She went on. "Luigi, José—Lucianna is going out of her mind. I'm coming in. Tell your friends to hold their fire."

A shout in Spanish echoed from inside. The commander turned to her. "They say it's OK for you to come in. Talk sense into them while you're in there. Tell them we're authorized to use any level of force to bring the situation to an end. And we really don't want it to come to that.''

''Well, *you* hold your fire and get those owners here. Talk sense into them. They'd better be ready to negotiate, and be very generous with it, if they want to take back anything worth having!''

She held the man's eyes until he nodded, then she rushed to retrieve her emergency bag. In seconds she was walking into the factory, her legs wavering beneath her. Armando hadn't called back. Oh, Lord, please—*please*!

As she entered, the tear gas made her choke, had her tears running faster. Then arms were sweeping her upstairs and away from the contaminated area. She stumbled, blind, panting, for two floors. Then at last she took a breath that didn't burn. And it hit her. His scent. *Armando!*

''What in heaven's name are you doing here, Laura?''

Her tears were a deluge by now. But blurred and distorted though he was, he was here, alive, standing, sounding...feeling strong and unharmed.

''Why did you come? How? Are you OK?''

He was holding her at arm's length, anxious eyes inspecting her for injuries. Hers did the same. Blood smeared a path from his temple over his cheek to his collar. Her trembling hand shot out, parting the matted hair. The gash was still bleeding. His hand clutched hers, drew it away.

''It's just a scalp injury—did it myself, too, on a broken window as I got in. Now, *por Dios*, answer me!''

''I'm here to save you. What else, Salazar?'' Her chuckle was hysterical with relief. ''Now, let me stitch this cut.''

''Forget it. I've got two gunshot casualties back there, one a direct bullet to the chest, the other from shrapnel flying off a window and hitting the shoulder, severing the axillary artery.''

''Oh, God. What did you do?''

''The axillary artery injury, that's Luigi, is stable now, with direct pressure to the wound and aggressive fluid replacement but it's the chest injury that's really scary. He needs an immediate thoracotomy to control his hemorrhage.''

"Then let's get him out of here.''

He shook his head. "The workers are convinced the police will open fire the moment they come out. From the unwarranted level of force so far employed, I can't say I blame them.''

"No, they won't. The new army commander on site said he doesn't want to do that.''

"Even so, that man won't last the trip to La Clínica. We have to do it here, now. I was trying to instruct others how to help me, but now you're here…''

"Let's do it!''

He didn't waste another breath.

"When was the last time you did a thoracotomy, Laura?'' Armando said as they prepped the man for the emergency procedure and laid out their instruments.

"In a factory? Never. You're doing it. I'm here to provide anesthesia, supportive measures and to revive you if you faint.''

He huffed a chuckle as she injected the unconscious intubated man with a muscle relaxant in lieu of anesthesia. "You don't have a rib-spreader with you by any chance, do you?''

"I didn't go that far preparing my kit. Next time I will.''

"Next time you'll need something else you didn't think to include!''

Then it began. He performed a left-sided thoracotomy to open the chest wall, an incision running from the breastbone to the mid-axillary line, cut through the intercostals, the ribs' muscles, then looked at her. "Care to act as the absent rib-spreader?''

Without hesitation she dipped her gloved hands into the operating field, spreading the ribs apart for him to reach the source of the bleeding, her arms trembling with the tremendous effort of keeping the tough bones apart.

In minutes, he'd cut off the bleeding lung lobe, sutured the thoracic aorta, gaining hemorrhage control. "Good man. He's fighting along with us. But we'll have to fish out the bullet later. He's stabilizing now, so let's close him up. I hope you have more fluids, massive doses of antibiotics and tetanus toxoid. I used mine up on the other injuries before this one happened."

After they'd finished up, Armando looked at her. "Now, about saving me. Have you cut a deal with the commander out there? Anything I can tell the people in here?"

She detailed the exchange. "Hmm." He frowned, then turned to the men who'd gathered round them to watch the impromptu operation on their friend in horrified fascination. "OK, men, we *may* be in a negotiating position. What are your demands? And please, make them within range of the acceptable. We want to keep your rights *and* get you home in one piece to your families."

The angry, desperate men's voices rose, impossible for Laura to understand. Armando clearly did.

At length, he turned to her. "Since you're the only one free to go in and out, can you tell them I want to act as negotiator?"

"I'll tell them *we're* acting as negotiators!"

His long look melted her down to her last cell. "Lead the way, then!"

"I can't believe it's over, just like that!"

Lame, Laura cursed herself inwardly, *lame and squeaking!* She gulped down another steadying breath as she placed the last suture in Armando's scalp gash. It still had no effect.

Oh, why had he insisted on going home after they'd managed to end the crisis? He'd left the rest of the trauma team to deal with their casualties, insisting he didn't need stitches, forcing her to chase after him...

Was there no limit to her powers of self-delusion? She'd chased after him because she'd been unable to do anything else. Because she had to be with him, talk to him, beg his forgiveness.

Not much chance of doing any of that while she was hyperventilating this way.

But it wasn't just being with him, it was being back home— *home*! The only home she'd ever known. The only home she ever wanted to know. It had nearly killed her walking out of here, walking away from him. Her emotional wounds were still open and bleeding.

Armando was answering her stupid comment. "It isn't over, and I doubt it will be any time soon." He rose, inspected the line of neat stitches amongst his clipped hair, then turned to her.

She didn't want to talk, she just wanted to be back in his arms. But she owed him. She had to pay her dues first.

"Armando, I came after you today—"

"To repay the debts you believe you owe me," he completed for her.

"I *do* owe you. You saved my life, more times than I can count. But that wasn't why— It wasn't!" she cried, when his gaze grew dismissive, disbelieving. "I also owe you more apologies than I can express. I as good as accused you of being a fraud, an abuser and— Oh, God, Armando, there's nothing more unjust, more stupid. You're so noble, so self-sacrificing that my accusations should be laughable instead of insulting. And I—I…"

Suddenly she heard echoes of the bullet screaming by her head. A shudder racked her. She could have easily died, without saving him, killing her baby. But the horrible waste would have been that she would have died estranged from him.

Touch him. She had to touch him. She did, ran her hands over his face, down his chest, with all her regret and frustration and love. He didn't even hesitate. He hauled her to him, fusing their mouths in a frenzy beyond desperation, growling for more, more. She gave him everything, begged for it.

"*Amor*, naked—have to have you naked, against me,

around me…'' His words, his feel, taste combusted her. Her hungry moans rose, the cold unfelt as her clothes gave way beneath his frenzied hands. He tore his own away, and she pounced on his beloved flesh, worshiping.

"Later, *amor*!" He carried her, laid her back on the dining table, spread her thighs over his hips, opened her, then took her. Took her home. Brought her to instant security, instant fulfillment.

Without breaking their union, he carried her shuddering and gasping up to their bed, her rounded belly nestled against his flat one. This time, his lovemaking was a possession. He laid her back, kneeled between her thighs, his face supernatural in beauty, all hunger and passion and potency, driving inside her with a gentleness and fullness that brought her to a climax that left her sobbing. Then higher, fiercer as she felt his own release inside her, heard his roars of completion and surrender.

After that she lost track of the intimacies he imposed on her and she demanded from him. Never before. Even through all the glory, never this profound, this total.

This had to be love's difference. Maybe he'd come to realize he loved her when he'd almost lost her. Yes, that had to be it.

Satiated, soothed, she slept, then woke many times. Then she woke one last time—not to his loving this time but to a wrenching loss.

It was morning. And Armando was leaving her.

He's just getting out of bed, moron, a reasonable voice sighed. *He does have to move some time, go to the bathroom or something.*

Then insecurity got a hearing. *Oh, yeah? So why does he look so—cold?*

Armando felt cold—frozen. The fusion reaction that had fueled their night had been doused by reality. Reality said it had all just been an expected post-traumatic outlet. It might have also been a goodbye, closure.

Laura was leaving Argentina today.

Not that he blamed her for wanting to leave. She must be fed up with the hard life, the constant work and crises, the lack of luxuries she must have been used to. Fed up with him and his dependence.

He'd at least release her from that, so she'd go with a clear conscience.

"After we've showered," he started as he got out of bed. "I'll take you back to your hotel to collect your things. Don't worry about your car. I'll see about selling it, then I'll send you the money. When's your flight? Have you decided where you're going?"

He pressed the sight of her as she sat up in bed between the pages of his mind. But she was opening her mouth—no! He had a monologue to deliver. Any interruptions might break him down. "Not that it matters. You'll do a magnificent job wherever you go. I can now expand La Clínica without GAO's help, but I wouldn't have gotten that far without them, without *you*. I really can't thank you enough for all you've done. My country owes you so much. Anyway, I doubt we'll ever meet again, but I want you to know I wish you and your daughter every happiness."

There. All in one go.

Why wasn't she going?

She was getting up, coming near, a strange expression on her face. What was that intensity? She was reaching for him— *Dios*, no! He could take no more of this.

He was too late to get out of her reach. "I—I don't have to go now, y'know?" Her voice was husky from too many cries of pleasure. He gritted his teeth against their echoes, in his mind, in his flesh. "Wouldn't you like it if I stayed longer?" Ripe nakedness pressed against his and he recoiled, yanked on a pair of jeans.

A strange sound issued from her—a laugh? "Whatever happened to the man who said he'd never get enough of me, who spent the night making good on his word?" He put on a shirt and turned away before he roared the place down. She followed him, pressed herself to his back, rubbed her face where his heart almost crashed out of it. "Armando, when I turned down your—your offer, I must have been in shock, not knowing what I was saying. Now your—the no-strings affair sounds great!"

So that was it. She was so hooked on sex with him, she'd keep him around as her stud. For *longer*. But why did it feel as if she'd just shot him in the gut? Wasn't that what he'd offered to be last week, desperate to hang onto her any way he could, for any length of time?

No, he couldn't even consider it any more. Not and keep his sanity. And if he broke, maybe she'd really have reason to fear him then!

He had to end it now.

He couldn't move or talk. Could only pray she'd be the one to shrug and walk out. She didn't.

Laura stood there, disintegrating. She wasn't reaching him at all. She'd left it too late, depleted her attraction, her use to him. He wouldn't have her on any basis. She would have groveled if it would have made a difference. One look at him said it wouldn't. And she just had to know. *Why?* Going insane with grief and rejection would come later—now she just had to have some concrete facts.

Anger and desperation would no longer be denied. "What was last night all about, then? Post-traumatic stress or one for the road? Why did you marry me in the first place? Not for the baby, that's for sure! So what has it been? To make sure GAO remains here long enough? Or has it been the sex? But even that's palled now, hasn't it? Or maybe it's been the money you thought I have—when I have nothing!"

Armando stared at her. He had no defenses against her power over him, against her accusations. She'd gotten the first two reasons right. At least at the very beginning. And if only sex or anything else had palled. But to be her lover, counting the days until she left him again and— Wait, she'd said she had nothing. But Diego had told him…!

His explosion stunned him as hard as it did her. "You can even consider I was after your *money*? *Dios!* That's too much. *Too much.*" His roar came to an abrupt end, dropping to a strident, bass whisper. "It's a good thing I turned down your generous offer. I don't want a woman who thinks me a mercenary bastard, not even for temporary sex!"

Laura watched his face close on final rejection as he went out, returning in seconds with her clothes and dropping them on the bed. "You'd better leave now, Laura. I'll send the signed divorce papers to GAO so they'll forward them to you, wherever you end up."

No. Even if it was over, she couldn't let it end this way. She had to set him straight, couldn't leave him in any doubt of what he was in her eyes. "Armando, please…" He turned away, his face contorting, his eyes shimmering. Tears? She'd hurt him *that* much? She cried out, her voice raw and wounded. "I beg you, let me explain! My doubts had nothing to do with you! It was my own insecurities…"

He lurched away when she touched his hand, and she clung, shaking, choking, tears streaming. "Just let me tell you— please, Armando!"

He still didn't look at her, but stopped fighting her off. A chance. She had to make it work. Her life depended on it.

"You know of my father, don't you? After he founded the Burnside Foundation and amassed a staggering fortune, he turned to aid work and left it in his beloved wife's—my mother—hands. Then he died during an expedition when I was eight, and she promptly remarried, the man she'd always wanted, his best friend. She and I were never close, but after that man was there, it was horrible. He systematically put me down, turned my mother against me. By the time my half-brother and -sister were born, I was treated almost as an enemy.

"I admit I made it very difficult for anyone to even tolerate me then, but I was a child, crying out for attention, for security. But the damage was done, and when her stud husband convinced her *their* children deserved the money, not the difficult daughter of the man she'd despised, she agreed. I've had to make my way through life since I turned sixteen. The most I've had was some good people not slamming doors in my face out of respect for my father's memory. Yet everyone has always assumed I was an heiress. Diego included.

"But I wouldn't have blamed you if my main attraction *had* been my non-existent fortune. You would have done great things with it, and I'm only sorry I have nothing to offer but my own two hands…"

Those hands cupped his face, flailed when she felt the moisture there. "Oh, Armando, I don't want to leave. Argentina is my home now—I want it to be my daughter's too."

Armando was reeling. What did it all mean? That she was sorry for misjudging him, still wanted him and loved Argentina? What about loving *him*?

It made no difference. If only she promised to stay for ever, he'd love for both of them.

He had to talk, manage something like real speech. His life depended on it. "I understand your fear for your daughter now—and I never explained how I feel. It's just so hard to make words describe it…"

They had to. "I've let my intense wish to be the one in your heart, the other half of your baby, cloud my mind—with pain, with longing for what might have been but wasn't. But not with hatred. *Dios*, this still doesn't sound right!"

He drove his fingers through his hair, steadying his thoughts, organizing their transformation into words. "I never really hated Diego. I loved him in a way, warts and all, and who doesn't have them? But whatever I felt or didn't feel for Diego has no bearing on my feelings for *our* baby. Please, please, believe that. I love and want her, if only you'll let me be her father. She could be the devil's own and I'd still love her. She's *yours* and that's enough. That's everything. And I—I don't want you to forget Diego, just to love me, too. If you can."

His impassioned words rang in the silence. He'd bared his soul and was standing there, exposed, vulnerable, awaiting her verdict.

And it was there all over her face, running down her cheeks, too incredible to believe—indescribable. Joy. Adoration. Pure, total. And it was for him. For him!

She launched herself at him. "Oh, Armando, I only ever loved you. Even when I thought I was loving Diego, I was loving *you*!" His confusion must have been all over him for she hugged him harder, her laugh the very sound of absolute happiness. Then she explained. "Diego spent a year online with me, telling me everything you would say, answering my questions the way you would, reciting your values, your jokes, even your speech patterns. I fell in love with the persona he projected, and he'd been projecting you. The poor man really had a huge hero-worship complex—and who could blame him?" She broke off to nip his chin, her smile almost stopping his heart with its beauty, its promise.

She went on. "But he was also very astute. After meeting me only once, he knew you were the one man I'd fall for. I don't appreciate the way he used that knowledge to trap me into getting involved with him, but I soon realized he was nothing like he pretended, nothing like you."

Anger erupted inside Armando, then just as abruptly dissipated, understanding replacing it. "He must have also realized you were the one woman I could want, since he delighted in rubbing my nose in it. But I can't even feel bad about what he did now. I can really sympathize with him for wanting you so much, he'd have done anything to get you. Just look at the lengths I went to. And another thing in his defense—he *was* fond of luxury, and your supposed fortune must have been an added attraction in his eyes, but I believe he'd still have wanted you no matter what."

He paused, frowned as all the missing pieces fell into place. "So, the villa, the reporters—all his doing?"

Her eyes grew thoughtful. "I can only guess at the reporters. Come to think of it—probably. As for the villa, I was shocked out of my mind when I came here and he told me how much my accommodation had cost him. I paid him back, believing he'd been swindled, wondering how I'd survive on GAO's meager salary. Then I saw the villa and knew why it had been so exorbitant. He really believed I could afford it easily. I tried to get my money back and...you know the rest!''

''And when Señor Delgado paid you back the rent, you kept a few hundred dollars to pay your bills, didn't you?'' She nodded and he sighed, ''Oh, Diego!''

Her similar sigh on their first night together, and that cry in her sleep on their wedding night, hit him again. He asked her, he just had to. She told him how wrong his interpretations had been.

Security, relief shook him, swept him. He let go of all his tension. He stroked her upturned face, drowned again in her beauty, in her love. Could he really be so blessed? ''*Mi amor*, if it wasn't for Diego, you would have never picked Argentina of all places to come to, and we would have never met. I would have never known you, known what life is all about. So not only am I not angry with him, I owe him a debt I can never repay. If only he was alive so I could at least try!''

''Oh, my love. I owe as much and more. And we'll find a way, believe me.'' She buried her face in his chest, breathed him in, nibbled at his buttons. ''And to think all my colleagues thought me crazy for joining GAO! Just look where and what it's gotten me. But my role with GAO is done—now my life-long role is with you. If you'll have me. And our daughter.''

He looked down at her, the most beautiful woman ever created, his woman, returning his love, fueling it, for ever. He took off his shirt, stopped her from helping him, took her lips in deep, abiding abandon. She sank on the bed, taking him with her. He molded her back to his front, and just before he joined them, taking her to their private place in heaven, he whispered in her ear, ''I'll show you if!''

Your opinion is important to us!

Please take a few moments to share your thoughts with us about Mills & Boon® and Silhouette® books. Your comments will ensure that we continue to deliver books you love to read.

To thank you for your input, everyone who replies will be entered into a prize draw to win a year's supply of their favourite series books*.

1. There are several different series under the Mills & Boon and Silhouette brands. Please tick the box that most accurately represents your reading habit for each series.

Series	Currently Read (have read within last three months)	Used to Read (but do not read currently)	Do Not Read
Mills & Boon			
Modern Romance™	❑	❑	❑
Sensual Romance™	❑	❑	❑
Blaze™	❑	❑	❑
Tender Romance™	❑	❑	❑
Medical Romance™	❑	❑	❑
Historical Romance™	❑	❑	❑
Silhouette			
Special Edition™	❑	❑	❑
Superromance™	❑	❑	❑
Desire™	❑	❑	❑
Sensation™	❑	❑	❑
Intrigue™	❑	❑	❑

2. Where did you buy this book?

From a supermarket ❑ Through our Reader Service™ ❑
From a bookshop ❑ If so please give us your Club Subscription no.
On the Internet ❑

Other _____ _____/_____

3. Please indicate by number which were the 3 most important factors that made you buy this book. (1 = most important).

The picture on the cover ___ I enjoy this series ___
The author ___ The price ___
The title ___ I borrowed/was given this book ___
The description on the back cover ___ Part of a mini-series ___

Other _____

4. How many Mills & Boon and /or Silhouette books do you buy at one time?

I buy ___ books at one time ❑
I rarely buy a book (less than once a year) ❑

5. How often do you shop for any Mills & Boon and/or Silhouette books?

One or more times a month ❑ A few times per year ❑
Once every 2-3 months ❑ Never ❑

6. How long have you been reading Mills & Boon® and/or Silhouette®?
_____ years

7. What other types of book do you enjoy reading?

Family sagas eg. Maeve Binchy   ❑
Classics eg. Jane Austen   ❑
Historical sagas eg. Josephine Cox   ❑
Crime/Thrillers eg. John Grisham   ❑
Romance eg. Danielle Steel   ❑
Science Fiction/Fantasy eg. JRR Tolkien   ❑
Contemporary Women's fiction eg. Marian Keyes   ❑

8. Do you agree with the following statements about Mills & Boon? Please tick the appropriate boxes.

	Strongly agree	Tend to agree	Neither agree nor disagree	Tend to disagree	Strongly disagree
Mills & Boon offers great value for money.	❑	❑	❑	❑	❑
With Mills & Boon I can always find the right type of story to suit my mood.	❑	❑	❑	❑	❑
I read Mills & Boon books because they offer me an entertaining escape from everyday life.	❑	❑	❑	❑	❑
Mills & Boon stories have improved or stayed the same standard over the time I have been reading them.	❑	❑	❑	❑	❑

9. Which age bracket do you belong to? Your answers will remain confidential.

❑ 16-24   ❑ 25-34   ❑ 35-49   ❑ 50-64   ❑ 65+

THANK YOU for taking the time to tell us what you think! If you would like to be entered into the **FREE prize draw** to win a year's supply of your favourite series books, please enter your name and address below.

Name: _____
Address: _____
_____
Post Code: _____ Tel: _____

Please send your completed questionnaire to the address below:

READER SURVEY, PO Box 676, Richmond, Surrey, TW9 1WU.

* Prize is equivalent to 4 books a month, for twelve months, for your chosen series. No purchase necessary. To obtain a questionnaire and entry form, please write to the address above. Closing date 31st December 2004. Draw date no later than 15th January 2005. Full set of rules available upon request. Open to all residents of the UK and Eire, aged 18 years and over.

As a result of this application, you may receive offers from Harlequin Mills & Boon Ltd. If you do not wish to share in this opportunity please write to the data manager at the address shown above. ® and ™ are trademarks owned and used by the owner and/or its licensee.

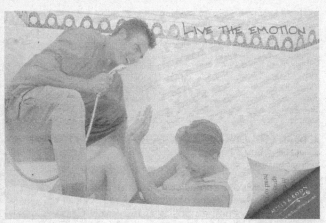

MILLS & BOON®

Live the emotion

0904/03b

_MedicaL
romance™

THE SURGEON'S FAMILY WISH *by Abigail Gordon*

Dr Aaron Lewis is captivated by new paediatric surgeon
Dr Annabel Swain—especially since she's saved his
daughter's life! He senses that Annabel, like him, has
lost a loved one and is longing for a family. He's
determined to help her overcome her past—but first
he has to convince Annabel to share her secrets…

CITY DOCTOR, OUTBACK NURSE *by Emily Forbes*

Flight Nurse Lauren Harrison was stunned when flying
doctor Jack Montgomery walked back into her life, six
months after their brief affair. Attending medical
emergencies together made it impossible for Jack and
Lauren to deny their attraction—but for Lauren the
question now is, how long would this city doctor last in
the Outback?

EMERGENCY: NURSE IN NEED *by Laura Iding*

Past feelings are reawakened for critical care nurse
Serena Mitchell when her ex-fiancé, Detective Grant
Sullivan, is brought into the trauma room. She broke off
their engagement when he refused to quit his
dangerous job—and now her fears have been proved
right. But caring for Grant is difficult for Serena – does
she still have feelings for him?

Don't miss out…

On sale 1st October 2004

*Available at most branches of WHSmith, Tesco, ASDA, Martins,
Borders, Eason, Sainsbury's and all good paperback bookshops.*

FREE!

4 Books
and a surprise gift!

We would like to take this opportunity to thank you for reading this Mills & Boon® book by offering you the chance to take FOUR more specially selected titles from the Medical Romance™ series absolutely FREE! We're also making this offer to introduce you to the benefits of the Reader Service™—

- ★ **FREE home delivery**
- ★ **FREE gifts and competitions**
- ★ **FREE monthly Newsletter**
- ★ **Exclusive Reader Service offers**
- ★ **Books available before they're in the shops**

Accepting these FREE books and gift places you under no obligation to buy, you may cancel at any time, even after receiving your free shipment. Simply complete your details below and return the entire page to the address below. You don't even need a stamp!

YES! Please send me 4 free Medical Romance books and a surprise gift. I understand that unless you hear from me, I will receive 6 superb new titles every month for just £2.69 each, postage and packing free. I am under no obligation to purchase any books and may cancel my subscription at any time. The free books and gift will be mine to keep in any case.

M4ZEF

Ms/Mrs/Miss/Mr ....Initials.......................................

BLOCK CAPITALS PLEASE

Surname ....

Address...

....

....Postcode ....

Send this whole page to:
UK: FREEPOST CN81, Croydon, CR9 3WZ